When Angels Walk the Earth

by
VL Parker

Verna-Lynn Parker.

VL Parker

Copyright © 2013 Verna-Lynn Parker
All rights reserved World wide

WORKS BY V.L. PARKER

To Hell & Back: A Test of Faith
February, 2012

To Hell & Back Book II: When Angels Walk the Earth
November 2014

To Hell & Back Book III: Final Conflict
To Be Released

To Hell & Back Book IV: The Secret of Jehovah
To Be Released

Chains Around My Soul: Between Shadows & Light, is a short compilation of the original poetry of VL Parker published, May 15 2013

ACKNOWLEDGMENTS

I have many people to demonstrate my appreciativeness to for enabling me to publish this work. I would like to thank Robert Parker for editing my first novel, **To Hell & Back: A Test of Faith.** I am very grateful to, Sarah and Jessica Parker. You have my gratitude for your time and feedback during the editing process. Matthew Parker aided with the cover design and also has my heartfelt appreciation. These novels would not have been complete without your support and assistance.

Finally, I thank my God, my Creator and Father, for all that he has blessed me with and for enabling me to write and share my creative works with the world. In all that I do, help me honor you with my art and my life.

DEDICATION

I dedicate this novel to all those who have the courage to stand up and fight injustice, and sacrifice to defend our freedom.

I also dedicate this novel to my husband Robert, who has showed me what love is. Thank you for loving me and accepting me for who I am, while inspiring me to grow.

Table of Contents

Prologue 5

Chapter One: Warrior of God 10

Chapter Two: New Life 52

Chapter Three: When Angels Come to Call 92

Chapter Four: In the Dark of the Night 102

Chapter Five: A Deeper Understanding 129

Chapter Six: United 141

Chapter Seven: The Eye of the Storm 169

Chapter Eight: In Enemy Hands. 193

Chapter Nine: Sacrifice 223

Chapter Ten: Angels and Demons 242

Chapter Eleven: In the Hands of God 275

About The Author 289

When Angels Walk the Earth

Prologue

I have been to Hell and back and now I walk between two worlds. I walk alone even though I am surrounded by those who love me and those who would die to protect me. I have survived death, but how will I survive life? I cling to hope and faith in better days to come.

I get flashes of memory of the repeated rapes and molestations; and it almost destroys me. I am sure that I would not have the strength to deal with that reality, that violation, if the memories of it were clear. Thankfully the drugs that they gave me prevent me from fully recounting the horrors I suffered. If I can survive the flash backs of Hell, I can survive anything, yet I am filled with rage and vengeance. Darkness clings to me, tearing at the fragment of my mind and poisoning the peace that used to reside in my soul.

I have never kept a journal before. I don't know why I have decided to keep one now, except to explore the shadows of evil that permeates my thoughts. They haunt me. I must be my own counselor, for no one else can understand what I have suffered. I walk alone.

Prayer has become more difficult. I used to hear God so plainly, but now his voice is distant and Wisdom is seldom heard, she too has remained silent. I don't know why she has been indiscernible for so long. Still, I will pray. I will write this journal for me.

I hope no one ever reads it, for they may see the fury that I battle within. It could be used against me, should I speak candidly. Dare I be honest, even with myself? I have no one to be open and truthful with, no one to pray with, and no one who could possibly fathom my predicament.

Ever since I was raped, I feel a hatred of my flesh growing inside of me. Sometimes I still have horrid dreams where I am being victimized and I'm helpless, unable to defend myself. I'm weak.

The dreams of Hell still haunt me too but I'm thankful that the demons have been silent in my waking hours, a brief reprieve. When I am lucid, I know that they are just dreams and yet, I have an urge to cut myself. I often wake clutching my knife.

Sometimes as I sit by the fire sharpening it, seeing the beauty of the blade glisten in the moonlight, I once again entertain thoughts of self-mutilation, but I don't act on them. I am still in control.

Still, when I have nightmares where I am sensual, I escape my slumber hating myself even more. I have longed to thrust my knife deeply into this putrid flesh and cut out the cancer in my soul. I need to make the darkness disappear.

I know it is the Devil, and the darkness inside of me escaping when I sleep. It oozes from my soul like a festering wound that cannot be healed. For far too long now I have come to hate slumber. Days go by when I don't rest at all. I don't want to close my eyes, lest my nightmares and the ill effects they have upon my psyche grow and consume my conscious thoughts as well.

Thank God I am strong when the morning comes. I am able to fight and to reason. I will not let Satan win. I only wish God were not so distant. No one would understand if I confessed. I can't share my darkness. I will simply have to battle it and win.

I feel the child growing inside of me and I am comforted knowing his destiny. I remind myself that he is a part of me and formed by the hand of God. I will focus on the light.

Peter cannot understand my faith. It is madness to him. He does not understand that I fight not only against flesh and blood, but also against a spiritual realm he cannot see, let alone fathom.

I envy him for that sometimes. He only accepts what he can see and touch with his own hands. His rational is concrete, and free from spiritual darkness. Peter is not attacked in his dreams. He is not plagued by demons.

Sometimes they try to slip into the community disguised as an animal, or even a human. They think they can infiltrate my camp and I will not see them. Fools, I have been granted sight. I sense a person's darkness before they ever open their mouths.

At first I cast the demons out, but now I simply kill them. I am so tired of this war, of this spiritual obscurity. Jacob told me to tread carefully in choosing what I kill and what I cast out. I used to know which course to take, but no more. I battle the evil single-handedly, unaided by the Spirit that used to guide me. Why is Heaven silent?

I use to try to spare the human's life, but lately I have sensed myself hardening and becoming more callous. The possessed are not saved souls, they are open to the legions of Demons stalking the Earth seeking residence.

I don't know why God has failed to let me know what I should do next. Perhaps it's the pregnancy. Maybe I am supposed to step back from battle and protect this child.

I am thankful for the fleeting moments of spiritual bliss that I am privy to. They, in part, sustain me. I relish when God's voice is clear and his counsel heard, but in times of distance, in times of silence, when all we have is our past experiences with God to hold onto, we must fight to keep our faith alive. In these dark days when the enemy wins and evil rises, our faith is tested most fervently. Here is where we must cling to hope.

I take it back; I don't envy Peter. Yes, I must battle evil, but it is always better to know the truth. To live in blindness and illusion would be unbearable. How do they survive without God? How do they retain their sanity when evil surrounds them, masked in the actions of malicious men?

No, without God sustaining me, I would have cut myself long ago. I would have killed myself when they ravaged me. Without God I would have lost all hope, and I would never have known love.

Peter is my only human love, my only way of grounding my-self in the light of day. When he holds me in his arms, my hope, my joy is rekindled and the darkness in me is diminished.

He once told me that, "Love heals all wounds." Peter believes that there is nothing that love cannot heal. He's right. God is love and he will heal us both. Peter and I love each other, and our human love is a beautiful reflection of the heart of God.

I see now why people keep journals; they express their menacing thoughts, helping to expel them like poison from the mind. They face their truth with naked transparency and then they are free to focus on their hopes, their dreams, and face the day with anticipation.

I will keep it and I will write and reflect. I only hope that the darkness does not rule me. I must remind myself that, although spiritually I walk alone, I am blessed to have Jacob, my angel, by my side and walking with me on my mission.

I am so thankful that I have Peter, my love. His love is tangible and loyal. I am not alone and even though I don't feel God lately, I know he is always with me and he will never leave me.

*****

Chapter One: Warrior of God

Peter and I were together and we were safe, but for how long, I didn't know. Satan had declared to the entire world that he was god of all mankind and he had recently announced that the people could worship him as Lumen.

Lumen meant Light in Latin. Lucifer was trying to regain his throne as Prince of this Earth. He was cast down from the highest heavens long ago. No longer able to sit with the gods as the Angel of Light, he claimed the Earth as his own, but God had other plans. He had allotted this planet for mankind to tend, until his son took his seat to rule and reign over all the Earth.

The Devil was determined to get it back. He viewed this realm as his kingdom, and humanity as his slaves. The dictator Augustus was ordered by Satan to find me, and he issued an edict to locate me at any cost.

I think they foolishly believed that if they could kill me and claim my son as their own, then they would win the war and crush the rebellion. They had no understanding of the tenacity of mankind and the beauty and resolve of free will. I was only one leader in this world wide rebellion against evil and we were determined to regain our freedom.

Regional governments across the globe demanded that all resources be used to find me and they labeled me, 'The Enemy of Peace'.

I was surprised to hear later from Eric, my chief computer technician and communications officer, that part of my escape from the insane asylum had been caught on camera and that someone leaked it through the Internet.

My escape was apparently celebrated by a select few and an embarrassment to others. The government would have preferred that my escape remain private, however they used their propaganda machine to demonstrate what a dangerous and well-trained insurgent I was.

Needless to say Sergeant Sayid, my first officer, and Jacob my personal guardian were also labeled as traitors. Peter was caught on camera too, but he was in disguise and was he not correctly identified. A photo of his face with his false identification, as Doctor Joshua Noll, was placed beside ours and he was labeled, an enemy of the state.

I wasn't afraid of being captured. Augustus had been urging Lumen to disband ARON, the Alliance Republic of Nations, due to the growing dissention within. Countries were turning against themselves as resistance to the New Order was rising again. Rebel groups within most realms resisted the emergence of dictatorship and the elimination of personal rights and freedoms, while politicians attempted to secure their seats of power and maintain influence in the New World Order.

The political chaos covered the globe in a blanket of shadows and intrigue. No one could be trusted at any level of government. Augustus and Lumen maintained their influence, but the Devil's power was only as potent as mans' willingness to submit to him.

Still, hope remained, for the free will of man was a far greater weapon than I ever imagined.

I once believed that the Devil couldn't do anything that God did not allow. Now such foolish beliefs sicken me. My experience has taught me otherwise. In a war no one is in control and chaos reigns, it is then that evil can experience a victory, unless good men and woman rise up to halt the depraved from advancing.

I now realize that it is Free will, choice, our actions and reactions that determines our destiny. I know good and evil whisper, influencing humanity, nudging them through the gateway of the eyes, the ears, the mind and our own selfish desires, in order to moves us in either direction. Still, in the end it is our decision, our will to act, react or do nothing.

This is the worst of all decisions, to do nothing, to say nothing, to sit idle by as chaos reigns, freedom is lost and malice and brutality tolerated. I could never remain silent in the face of evil. No, it is up to those who are virtuous to battle, and when necessary, destroy the wicked.

*****

Last night I was plodding along the river. Jacob walked faithfully a few steps behind, watching over me, ever vigilant. I was thankful for my protector. However, he sensed that I needed my solitude so, instead of walking alongside me, he maintained his distance. He was close enough to defend me, but he kept plenty of distance between us, giving me the illusion of being alone.

My mind was restless tonight, as a tumultuous spirit was awakened and I couldn't figure out why. It was the essence of a warrior that stood ready to be released. I could not quiet my soul, and rage was slowly rising up within me.

Try as I may, I could not relax. So, I walked trying to sooth my uneasiness with the sounds of the water rushing by me. The river was loud and forceful and the winds began to blow, echoing my emotional state.

I did not know why I was being filled with an intensifying spirit of rage, but it was growing in power with every step I took. The farther I walked away from the main camp the more infuriated I became. I stopped to breathe in the cold mountain air, filling my lungs. This always had calmed me in the past, but not that night.

I heard a child crying, his wailing carried upon the wind. It called to me through the darkness. I made my way toward some caves nestled to the side of the mountain near the water.

I entered a cave and saw a child's face lit up by firelight. Tears streamed down his face and his eyes were filled with fury. I remembered seeing this boy before, when I entered the camp, after my incarceration. From the first moment I saw him I noticed his pain, but I did not know its depth or its source.

I identified him as a kindred spirit and I felt the ferocity inside of him, but I never investigated further to discover the cause, at least I didn't the last time I saw him.

He was the angry boy from our Karate class. I encountered him before my confinement in the insane asylum. He reminded me of myself at that age.

I hoped that I had helped him when I taught him to breathe properly, to recognize that peace is stronger than power. I still remember his graduation ceremony so vividly. This young warrior in training was attacking his target with rage...

Sayid stopped him, warning, "You must never fight with rage. Vengeance belongs to God. We must never take pleasure in killing, for then it becomes murder in our heart and our righteous action becomes tainted with sin.

We must remain calm and clear. Fury will interrupt your clarity of thought, which is one of the most important strengths in any battle. Furthermore, rage disrupts your breathing; so if you feel yourself losing control to anger or fear, take time to breathe deeply and slowly."

"Do you take time to breathe?" The boy asked.

Sayid knelt down and answered with his hand on the child's shoulder, "Yes, I always take time to pray and be still before Allah, seven times a day, but Catherine has taught me the value of breathing deeply. Catherine says that when she sits still and breathes, she not only rejuvenates her strength and spirit, she purifies her mind and hears from the creator himself."

"Do you hear from God, Sayid?" The boy inquired.

"Not at these times, but he speaks to me in dreams." Sayid replied.

"Then why take time to breathe deeply every day?" The boy asked.

"It enables you to breathe in battle when pain, anger, or fear takes control of you." Peter replied.

"Such discipline should become second nature to you, and then you will not succumb to panic." Peter added.

I had heard their conversation and I declared, "Breathing will also make you stronger than anger." The boy did not believe it, but after I showed him, he appeared to embrace the teaching.

I saw little of him after that, until I came back to camp. I noticed him training in the courtyard when I arrived the other day and he entered into every situation with a fury and the resentment of a wild tiger that was chained, held captive against its will. The boy often sat by himself, and he ate alone too.

That night I asked Sayid if he knew the boy's story and he informed me, "I forget his name, but he is one of the orphans. We have many in the camp and their numbers increase daily. He was one of the fortunate ones. It is sad that both of his parents were martyred, but at least he has a sister. His uncle took him in and brought them into our community. He should be thankful, unlike many other children here, he is not alone. He has family, people who love him."

I said nothing, but I watched the boy at a distance, knowing deep inside that he had a valid reason for his temper. Last night I discovered why, when I felt his wrath sweep over me as I approached a cave near the river.

I sensed him as I drew near. I heard and felt his anguish as the wind howled a painful lament and I saw his tortured face before me, illuminated by the small camp fire, flickering in the darkness.

Then I heard the voice of the boy crying, "Please don't. Please stop."

"Be quiet or I'll kill you." A man warned.

"Kill me now then." The boy sobbed.

"Be quiet and if you tell, or if you don't behave, I'll kill your sister and your friends as well, after I enjoy them." The vile man hissed.

"Not if I kill you first." I stated coldly as I emerged from the darkness.

The man stumbled back and the young boy, the child that broke the boards at the Karate training camp before my incarceration, recognized me when I entered the cave. He was definitely the angry lad that I had watched at a distance.

I remembered his uncle's face too. He had helped Mary teach the schoolchildren to read, write and do basic math and science. He was not possessed; but I sensed the wickedness within him nevertheless. I loathed him as much as I detested the Devil himself, perhaps more.

"Stay back or I'll break his neck!" The vile man shouted, as he took shelter behind the child.

"You won't have time, not before I break yours." I warned, devoid of all emotion.

He smiled and said with confidence, "Commander, you may be as good as a fighter as they say, but you couldn't possibly get to me before you hear the snap. Besides, rumor has it that you're a pregnant bitch. Are you willing to risk the life of your own baby to save the boy?"

"She can kill you, or I can. Now release the child, for I will show you far less mercy than she." Jacob stated as he stepped forth from the shadows.

'Not likely.' I thought, but I said nothing and I hoped that the boy would remember his training. He did.

The boy took a deep breath and stepped back towards the side of his attacker swiftly as he simultaneously grabbed the villain's elbow with his left hand. Then the boy quickly grabbed the degenerate's wrist, twisting it behind his back. Then, my young warrior, wrapped his left leg behind the pervert, forcing his knee to the ground, followed by a quick punch to his neck.

The boy then scrambled away as his uncle keeled over and Jacob and I quickly moved in. I ordered Jacob, "Take the lad outside!"

I kicked the man in the face as he was kneeling on the ground and I said, "Jacob was wrong." I smiled as I drew my knife, and I continued, "I will show you no mercy. I know God will send you to Hell and you will suffer greatly, but not before I make you pay in this world first."

I slashed his arm with my knife and I turned swiftly in the opposite direction, elbowing him in the head. I took a deep breath and calmed myself as I wiped a little blood splatter from my face and I said, "I must be careful and control myself. I don't want you to lose consciousness."

I kicked him in the ribs and I heard a crack as he screamed out in pain as I interrogated him probing, "How many children have you preyed upon, snake?"

"He was my first, I swear." He cried.

"Liar!" I grunted as I sliced his cheek followed by another elbow to the jaw in rapid succession as more blood sprayed through the air and sprinkled upon my forearm.

With a cold emotionless tone I continued, "I should cut out your tongue for lying."

He glared at me and dared to question, "Who are you to judge me? You murder, torture, and lead a rebellion against the state under the guise of being some sacred religious leader. You're a fucking hypocrite and a whore, living in sin with Roberts and having his bastard out of wedlock."

I shook my head and said, "Oh, there is so much you don't know about me. You see, I confess that I do judge you. I hate you. I promise that I'll make you suffer for the countless children you've abused. You will pay for the souls you murdered and the innocence you stole."

He stared up at me and shouted, "Shut-up Bitch!'

I kneed his face in response, and then I continued, "It may be considered murder that I am about to commit, but right now, I really don't give a shit."

He spit blood and cried, "You don't have the right to kill me. Your followers won't tolerate it. You claim to be called by God and yet you judge me. Fuck you."

I paced and knelt on one knee before him as I informed him, "I am not some sacred religious leader, maggot. I am a warrior of God. He saw fit to equip me with strength you cannot comprehend, and I will unleash that power on you."

"You self-righteous, little whore!" He spit.

He went to swing at me; I grabbed his wrist with ease and broke it. He screamed out in pain again and I cut his chest slowly with my blade, making sure not to cut too deeply as the blood oozed from his body and I whispered, "I am not a whore; the child within me was placed there by monsters like you."

He realized that his death was imminent and he continued to attack me the only way he could, with words. He sought to manipulate me, "You're such a fucking fraud. You're not torturing me because of that boy, or any of the other children. You want vengeance for what was done to you."

Fear shrouded his face once again and he added, "I was using your words, not mine. What's wrong did someone love you when you were young?"

I stuck my knife in his shoulder and twisted it as I spoke with venom, "Don't you fucking dare use that word again. You don't love. You use, you abuse and manipulate and you don't know anything about me, snake."

He screamed, cried, pleaded, and then conceded, "Please... you're right, you're right, I don't fucking know you. Please, stop!"

I pulled the knife out slowly and he held a shirt to his shoulder. Tears streamed down his eyes as he continued, "I can't help but think you are hurting me because what was done to you, not anyone else. Please let me go don't take your vengeance out on me. I wasn't the one who raped you."

"I do not take revenge for myself, snake, but something dark and powerful awakens within me when women, and especially children, are preyed upon by monsters like you. You didn't harm me, but you did rape others, didn't you?' I said with an edge of resentment in my tone as I forced restraint.

"No, no, I didn't I swear. They all loved me." He pleaded.

This enraged me further as I kicked him in the head. Then I leaped toward him as he lay upon the ground weeping, holding a knife to his throat I said, "I told you not to use that word again."

He sobbed, "What are you waiting for? Kill me already." He wept as I pulled him to his knees. He swayed back and forth as the pain was beginning to overwhelm him. Soon he would go into shock, but I wanted him to suffer more first.

I took another deep breath as I uttered, "Well that's tempting. I planned on it, but first I want you to pay for your crimes. Alas, I am not sure how much more you can handle. You're weak. Perhaps I'll let you heal, hold a public trial, and punish you again before I kill you."

I noted a flash of fear in his eyes. It was only momentary. I confess it gave me a little satisfaction, but it was not enough as he hissed, "Go to Hell!"

I leaned in and I whispered in his ear, "I have already been to Hell. Now it's your turn." I plunged my dagger into his abdomen and slowly twisted my dagger. He writhed in pain, his face twisted and gruesome. He gasped and drew his dying breath as Peter walked in. I pulled my knife from his body and I rose to face Peter, bathed in the vile creature's blood.

I stood up taking a deep breath and as I exhaled I felt a release. I was breathing easily as I walked away from the body, momentarily feeling as if a burden had been lifted and Peter asked, "What the hell is going on here?"

"Pedophile..." I answered bluntly and then I inquired, "Where's the boy?"

"He's with Jacob in our cave. I knew something was wrong when Jacob returned without you by his side. He told me you were here." Peter paused, "Is he dead?"

I nodded despite the stupid question. It was not like Peter to state the obvious, but I think he was in shock. I was drenched with the monster's blood and my demeanor disturbed him. I asserted. "At least we can take comfort in the fact that he will never hurt another child again."

"Are you okay?" Peter inquired tentatively.

"Yes." I replied, "Let's go check on the boy."

As we left the cave Peter questioned, "Catherine, did you have to kill him?"

"He deserved to die." I replied with a stern tone still wrestling with deep seated spirit of wrath that began to rise up again as Peter berated me.

"You should have had him stand trial and made an example of him before everyone else in the camp. Now no one will know for sure if he was guilty." Peter argued.

"He was guilty, he was caught trying to violate the boy, and I assure you it was not the first time, nor his first victim." I answered, not able to hide my fury as I glared at Peter and continued, "How can you defend such a wicked and vile creature?"

Peter grabbed my arm and made me stop and talk to him and he chastised me, "Don't be ridiculous Catherine, you know I would never defend such a thing. Hell, I probably would have nearly beaten him to death too, but you gutted him. That's murder, not justice. You appointed yourself, judge, jury and executioner. We can't allow something like this to happen again. We should have given him a trial before the people."

"Perhaps you're right Peter." I acknowledged, "But how would we sentence him? How would he serve out his punishment? We have no prisons, no means to ensure he doesn't escape and re-offend. No, for too many centuries men have been allowed to rape women and children with no real consequence."

I stared across the raging river and then I spoke again, "Peter, I remember once when a young man once stole my father's car collection and he had to serve out decades in prison for his crime. In that same era, if a man raped a woman, he wouldn't serve more than a few years. Do you remember what the sentence was when someone violated a child? They killed who that person was inside and all that they would be, and yet they served so little time. A pedophile doesn't just harm the child physically Peter, they kill a part of their soul and leave them crippled and weak, let alone feeling dirty, ashamed and defiled. Judges ordered them serve out a short sentence and then let them out into our communities again, where they could prey upon children once more? The court system was always claiming that they served their time. Well no longer, not under my watch, they will pay with their lives. "

I couldn't stop my tirade or quell the vengeance inside me as I ranted, "Men have tolerated such evil for far too long, these wicked men cannot be reformed, and the only answer is to kill them. It is the only way to protect the children." I was exasperated; I took a deep breath and tried to calm myself. It would have been easier if Peter would let up, but he didn't.

"Catherine, we can still ensure the sentence for such a crime is death, but we cannot be arbitrary about who should live and who should die. We need to bring them to justice, through proper channels, before the people. If we don't, we risk becoming like the very monsters we are fighting against. Think about it Catherine, what kind of world do you want to live in? Don't you want freedom, democracy and justice?" Peter asked me with a calm and pleading tone as he placed both of his hands upon my shoulders.

I thought for a moment and looked up at the sky, the stars and the full moon that shone brightly, reflecting on the surface of the water and then I turned to look up at him and I said, "Of course I want a world like that, but this monster was caught in the act Peter, and I can't risk allowing such a villain to get away and harm even one more child. He deserved to die and I don't regret killing him."

Peter said, "Freedom and justice has its costs Catherine. When men, or women, rule with absolute authority, the people cannot be free. Liberty and justice are all or nothing states, Catherine. Neither can be limited, they cannot be parceled by a ruler and portioned out as they see fit, or it ceases to exist. We must design a way to guarantee that justice is served and ensure that everyone has the right to an impartial judge. Defendants must stand trial before the people."

"As long as the children are not the ones to pay the price and the penalty for molesters and rapists will be death." I was adamant on this point, for in my mind, no pedophile deserved to live. Our children would not only be made safe, the world was a better place without such men, so I added, "We will honor the people's right to receive justice, but our primary objective will be to protect those who cannot protect themselves. There cannot be freedom without security Peter. The children have a right to feel safe."

Peter sighed, "Of course they do Catherine, but even your bible says that all sins can be forgiven, save one. What if reform were possible, what if your God did bring such a man to be filled with remorse. This is never going to happen if you kill such people without a trial, without an opportunity to..." I could tell that the words that came from his mouth were distasteful to him, but he said them anyways, "...to repent."

"Such men cannot be reformed and remorse is not repentance. Such men can't be...." I couldn't finish my sentence. I turned away from him. I knew I had put myself in the place of God. I was broken and angry, filled with such violence and rage that I could barely contain it.

I held my breath, and then sighed as Peter turned me gently back toward him and lifted up my chin to look in my eyes as he finished my sentence, "Forgiven. Your Savior says otherwise Catherine. Are you going to go against your own spiritual beliefs to satisfy your need for justice, for vengeance? I know you, Catherine. If you continue to follow this path, you will destroy yourself with shame and guilt. You could drive yourself mad with remorse, and bitterness."

I turned on him even though I knew he was right, I couldn't contain myself as I retorted, "If the LORD can save a man such as this then he better not let him enter my camp, and prey upon the children. If God does not protect them and take action, then I promise, I will."

Peter did not respond because in his heart he understood this feeling all too well. He was still angry with my God and now so was I.

Peter sighed, "You better wash some of that blood off yourself before you see the boy."

I knelt by the river and removed my over-shirt and rinsed it in the river. I washed my face and arms and used my shirt to wipe the knife clean. I sheathed the knife and dipped my shirt in the river again. I wrung it out and then we returned to the cave in silence.

When I entered the cave I saw the boy sitting by the fire with Jacob by his side.

He looked up and inquired, "Is he dead?"
"Yes." I replied
"Thank you." He said softly.

I held him and tears flowed from our cheeks, I wiped the tears from his face and stroked his hair softly. I then assured him with barely a whisper, "You're safe. He will never hurt you again."

I couldn't sleep and Peter stayed up with me and pulled me close to him. He caressed my hair and whispered, "He will heal Catherine. You saved him and because of that he will never forget what you did for him."

We both watched the boy sleeping as I reclined in Peter's embrace. All the stress washed away and serenity held me close, as I welcomed the exhaustion knowing that in that moment, I found peace.

*****

The boy slept soundly in my cave last night and in the morning I held a meeting and I addressed the camp as a whole. When they assembled I hiked up a nearby cliff, a hanging boulder near the river. Jacob, Sayid and Peter stood on the rock with me and our squad was below us facing the crowd.

I looked at the sea of people before me. There were too many to count, too many to keep track of. It was then that I was sure that the camp had to be made more manageable, and secure. We had to disband into smaller units.

The rebels and their families all stood before me, with the children in the front staring up at me as

I looked upon them with compassion. Then I spoke to the masses. I had resolve and my tone was firm and my wrath tempered only by the presence of the little ones...

The camp was silent and I declared, "You all know we live in very dark times. The Devil, the self-proclaimed god known as Lumen, Augustus and his soldiers are not our only enemies. We also must battle the enemy that lies within. Inside every one of us is a darkness and a light.

Sky once explained a Cherokee legend to me. It is called, 'The Legend of the Two Wolves'. Children, I want you all to listen carefully to this story and all that I am about to tell you."

I stepped down and crouched as I look upon the children with empathy as I continued, "A grandfather was teaching his grandchildren about life. He told them about a fight that was going on inside of him. This same war is waged inside each and every one of us. It is a terrible battle and it is between two wolves that dwell within our very souls.

One wolf is bad; we see him when we give into fear, anger, lament, or self-indulgence. It is filled with, pride, self-gratification, shame, hatred, inferiority, and deceit. This wolf is most ferocious when preying upon others.

The other wolf within us is good; this part of our soul is expressed in our joy, peace, love, hope, and in our sharing with one another. We see it expressed in our humility, compassion, generosity, friendship, honesty, faith and good deeds."

The boy who was abused last night spoke up and questioned, "What wins, the light, or the darkness?"

I replied, "One child asked his grandfather the same question, 'Which wolf will win?' Do you know how he answered?"

The boy shook his head, no.

Sky answered as he knelt down before the boy and placed his hand on his shoulder, "The one you feed."

I looked and spoke gently toward the children, my tone softened as I said, "Children, please forgive me for exposing some of you to things that you may have been unaware of, but knowledge is power. So, I want each and every child to know that no one, no matter who they are, has a right to hurt you. If anyone ever does anything to you that you feel is wrong, or hurts you, or makes you do something to them that you are not comfortable with, please talk to one of the commanders. We will protect you. Children you may go now."

As the children made their way toward breakfast Caleb remained seated as I continued to warn the adults, I stood tall and jumped back up upon the bolder, overlooking the masses as I announced, "Last night, I killed a pedophile caught in the act of molesting a child."

I remained silent for a moment as the camp seemed to collectively gasp and then some began to whisper, "Who could have done such a thing?" I held up my hand and waited for silence.

I continued with a powerful voice, "Be warned, if I ever find out that you are harming a woman, or a child, or any other being for your own evil, self-gratification; I will punish you immediately and without mercy. I have ordered my commanding officers to do the same. Any and all forms of sexual abuse will never be tolerated, or pardoned in our camps."

Some shuffled uncomfortably as I warned, "Know this, if any of you think that you can get away with seducing a child, you will not." I continued as I clutched the hilt of my knife, speaking in a low tone with my other fist clenched as I declared, "We will educate the children and we will continue to equip them for battle. They will be educated and encouraged to speak openly and honestly about any issue."

I removed my hand from my blade and relaxed my clenched fist a little, forcing myself to take deep breath before continuing, "We live in unruly times, and my heart is saddened knowing that the innocence of children has long been lost and now for they must know the evil in the human heart as well.

All issues addressed with them in the most age-appropriate manner, but we must ensure they are not ignorant of the truth and are aware of their rights. We will protect the children.

Whispers arose again among the adults and I lifted my hand and waited for silence a second time. I knew the wrath inside me was rising to the surface once again. My eyes glared at the men and women who stood before me, I could not help it. They fell silent, and I continued my tirade, "Jesus once said in scripture, '...better that you were never born, a millstone hung around your neck and you be thrown into the depth of the sea...' He warns those who lead a child into sin.

When we are divided into smaller camps my commanders will be ordered to kill any sexual abuser caught in the act. Anyone charged with the crime will be detained and placed on trial. Should they be found guilty the sentence will be death."

Peter caught my eye and he knew the depth of my rage, but he did not know how far I would go to avenge the murder of a child's soul. He was watching me with caution and I continued, "I too, battle the darkness within. I battle wrath and vengeance, and I am blessed that my darkness is always directed against evil. I control my fury, but I will let it loose on anyone who dares to hurt a defenseless soul."

I am small in stature compared to many of the men in my camp; still, they dared not look directly into my eyes. At this moment I sensed many feared me. I stated, "If any of you have the propensity toward committing such evil acts, I recommend that you leave our community immediately, for my men share this resolve."

I walked among the people as I warned them, "Know your darkness and feed the white wolf for those who feed the black one inside of you will not last long in this community. Dismissed!"

I walked past the crowd and marched toward the children as my men followed. Jacob and Peter pulled up alongside me.

Peter spoke to me in a hushed tone as everyone made their way toward breakfast, "Catherine, I'm worried about you; I have never seen you so..." He searched for the right words.

"Callous." I answered.

He nodded, but he remained silent, so I continued, "Peter, rarely have I ever been filled with this much fury, and wrath, I control it with a detached restraint, but you have caught a glimpse of it before."

He stopped and thought and then remembered as he said, "On the beach in Ireland, when those sailors tried to rape you and in the asylum."

"Yes, when they stabbed my dog and when they tried to seal me with the Devils mark." I said seething beneath my tempered state.

Peter said, "The microchip."

I replied, "Yes."

Peter noted, "You felt vengeance toward them, but the fullness of your ferocity isn't unleashed until another's harmed."

I nodded, "I'll eat breakfast first, but then I must go and wrestle with God. My anger is toward him as well. Do you understand?"

"I don't understand your faith most of the time, but in this, I certainly do. I felt it when your god allowed them to rape you. If he does exist, I hate him for allowing such a thing. Trust me, I understand." Peter countered.

"Well, I must deal with God and face this struggle, or I will be rendered useless to everyone. You were right, if I don't the darkness will consume me, and I will be changed forever." I confessed.

Sky walked up to us and informed me, "Commander, the boy wants to talk to you."

"What's his name?" I inquired as we made our way toward the breakfast tent.

Sky answered, "Caleb."

"Caleb, may we sit with you?" I asked. He was sitting alone, ashamed that everyone suspected he was the one abused. Gossip spreads fast and the camp knew that he slept in our cave last night. They also were aware that we didn't normally sit with children, so their suspicions were confirmed. He nodded and Jacob and I sat on either side of him. Sayid, Peter and Sky sat across from us.

Jason and Mary served us breakfast and then sat down too. We ate in silence and then I asked, "Caleb would you like to train with us after breakfast?" He was not ready to talk even though he wanted to. My encounter with God would have to wait. Caleb needed me and I would be patient and listen when he was ready.

Caleb nodded yes, but he did not say a word.

"Go get dressed for training and meet us at the obstacle course in about an hour, okay?" He nodded, still he did not speak, so I left to meet with my commanders and solidify their orders.

I would have to leave camp soon; my pregnancy was becoming visible. I knew I had to protect my child, but first I had to ensure that the other children would be safe in my absence.

I met with the squad leaders in the command tent after breakfast and before training. "Catherine we can implement your orders while we are here," Sayid stated, "but what do we do when we all leave on mission? We need to have someone in charge, a detachment left behind with each group."

I inquired, "Has anybody herd from Eric yet? "

"No, but Jason may have." Peter answered.

I ordered, "Go get him Sky, tell him we need him at this meeting immediately."

We waited for Jason to return with Sky and addressed the issue of the ever-growing number of cells, in the resistance. Despite the growing number of martyrs and the increased number of security forces within the cities, the résistance had survived and was managing to disable much of Augustus's communication network. He was increasingly forced to focus his attention to maintaining control of the cities leaving the people of the mountains free.

We needed new recruits for the resistance, but as the numbers within the camps grew the ability to train and ensure security diminished. Infiltration was always an issue, but now it was one of the most critical matters that lay before us.

"We need to find a history and profile on the best trained men and women in our camp. We need to identify any who have served in either, police, fire, or rescue operations, as well as identify those men and women with criminal records." I demanded.

Peter declared, "We don't have the capability, not living in the wilderness and caves, not without Eric and his network equipment. It's impossible."

Jason walked in and joined us, "Actually Eric didn't take all of his equipment with him. I have his passwords, but I don't know how he hacks into government satellites, or even how he accesses their networks." Jason noted.

"Hello Jason, have you heard from him at all?" I inquired.

"No, the last time he made contact he was on his way toward San Francisco to meet with a community of hackers. That was weeks ago. I haven't heard anything since." Jason shared.

I placed my hand on his and I said, "I'm sorry. God be with him."

Then Peter inquired, "What equipment did Eric leave behind?"

Jason replied, "He left two of his laptops and a thumb print scanner. He kept records of every new person to enter the camp, at least until he left. He has a spreadsheet on everyone, with skills and background checks, and another that is encrypted with all our plans, attacks and military contacts."

I grinned and said, "Eric is amazing."

"Sayid have your men gather information subtly concerning people's character. Our community has grown too large. Soon we will disband into smaller groups and we will train and appoint a force to protect the children when we leave. Meanwhile, you go with Jason and access those spreadsheets on the people in this camp." He complied immediately without a word.

****

My men were unusually silent in the meeting today
I think they feared me after the events of last night and my speech this morning. I couldn't blame them, I had no remorse or regret for my actions, but the power of that wrath was extensive and obvious to anyone who knew me.

We made our way to train where Caleb awaited our arrival and Sayid joined us and asked, "Caleb, are you ready to work hard?"

He nodded and stood tall as he answered, "Yes sir." So we began with a series of obstacle courses and martial arts training followed by hand to hand combat. Then I dismissed the men and said, "Caleb, the men have work to do, but Jacob and I are going to run up the mountain, do you want to come?"

Caleb nodded, but still said nothing. When we got to the top of the mountain we sat to meditate and breathe, Caleb did likewise.

I had a vision of the two wolves fighting, they were both strong and fearsome and the battle was intense.
The white one was victorious, and then the two wolves became one. The new wolf was even larger

and mostly black, however it had a white collar that covered its shoulders and chest and also had four white paws. The wolf was strong and fearsome, yet it was calm as the Lord approached it and pet it, rubbing its chest and then it howled and walked off, following the Lord.

The vision ended and I opened my eyes to see Caleb staring at me. I took a deep breath and stood up. Caleb asked, "Did you hear him? Did you hear from God?"

"No, but I saw him in a vision." I replied honestly.   Caleb asked me what I saw and I told him.

Caleb frowned and inquired, "What did it mean?"

I contemplated the vision for a moment and then I answered, "I think it means that both darkness and light still battle within me. They are both a part of me, but a day will come when the two shall become one, united in a new creation under the Lord's control. He tames the beast within. The wolf howled because he celebrated his freedom, a shout of praise that the battle was over.

Visions can be difficult to decipher, but never doubt that they are a message from on high."

Caleb shared, "I've never had a vision, or heard from God."

"There will come a day when you will." I assured him as we made our way back down the mountain.

"How do you know that?" Caleb questioned and I could hear the doubt in his voice.

I smiled, "Because I know God, and he named you well."

"What do you mean?" Caleb challenged

We stopped and looked at him; Jacob kneeled down on one knee and said, "Your name means, 'Bold' as well as, 'Faithful.' God is faithful and he will honor your courage and honesty Caleb. You will one day become a faithful warrior of God."

"Why should I be a warrior for God? He never defended me! He never protected me!" Caleb cried as tears streamed down his face.

I wept too and I knelt on one knee and wiped his tears as I said, "He did. He sent me to protect you Caleb. I failed you, I'm sorry."

"You didn't fail me, you killed him, and you did what I was too afraid to do. I wanted to kill him, I was trained to, but I was scared, weak and, and...I failed to protect myself. It's not your fault Commander." Caleb was so ashamed and angry at himself. I needed to get through to him.

I was resolute as I commanded, "Caleb it was not your fault, you have nothing to be ashamed of. It was that snake's evil, selfish and self-indulgent warped nature that is to blame, not you. It was never your fault."

"But how can you blame yourself Commander, you didn't know?" Caleb asked confused.

I felt guilty for not protecting him before and I questioned, "He has been abusing you since you broke that board last summer, perhaps even earlier than that, probably before I was arrested, right?"

Caleb looked hurt and betrayed as he asked me, "How did you know?

"I knew you had this rage, anger, and hurt inside you and I didn't once stop to ask you why. I should have investigated then. I failed you Caleb. I'm sorry, can you forgive me?" I pleaded.

"There is nothing to forgive Commander, I owe you everything. How can I ever repay you? You saved me." Caleb answered as he hugged me.

"You owe me nothing Caleb. I just wish I had killed him earlier. Who knows how many children I could have saved from his clutches?" I replied.

"Others..." Caleb was shocked as he inquired, "What others?"

"You're not alone Caleb, I guarantee that there are others. Predators never prey upon only one victim, sadly there are many. We must find them and help them heal. God forgive me for not protecting the children." I hated that this happened, especially under my command, and then I reminded myself, I was conversing with a child who desperately needed to feel safe.

I added, "Don't worry Caleb; you're safe now and I will do everything I can to make sure this never happens to a child in our community again."

Caleb questioned, "How, aren't you leaving us soon?"

I was brutally honest with Caleb as I confessed, "Yes, I have to, but my men now know the darkness that we allowed to creep into our camp and we will all be on guard against it. A police force is being formed and they will also watch over you and I will pray for you, for all of you."

"Why? I prayed for years and God did nothing. Why bother praying at all? Why didn't he protect me? I thought I was the only one, now I learn there may be many. Is he angry with us? Why didn't he protect us?" Caleb uttered in anger once again.

"I'm angry with God too, Caleb. I don't know why he allowed this evil to occur. I can't hide the anger that fills me when I think of what happened to you. I'm sorry, I don't have all the answers Caleb, but will you promise me this?" I pleaded

"What?" He sobbed staring down at the rushing river below, where we had stopped to talk.

"First, don't blame God for the evil that men do. Blame them. We are each responsible for our own actions and reactions." I pleaded.

I told him, "I have seen and heard God; I have been filled with his spirit of peace, love and joy. God is good Caleb, even though I too am angry with him, knowing that he is all powerful and yet does nothing to intervene, to protect when he should. I don't know why he doesn't, but I know God is good and he is love. Don't doubt that Caleb.

We must trust that justice will be served and that a day will come when he brings retribution, for the bible says, 'Vengeance is mine, declares the LORD!' That means he will ensure that there is a day of reckoning, Caleb." I realized I was talking to myself as much as I was speaking to Caleb.

Caleb understood most of what I was saying, but he questioned, "Reckoning, what's that?"

Jacob answered, "It is a day of, when mankind's' wrong actions will be called to account and weighed"

"It's like the statue of a lady I once saw in the city holding the scales of justice. Is that the day where your good deeds will be weighed against your bad?" Caleb asked with a touch of fear and distrust in his eyes. I could tell he did not want his perpetrator forgiven.

"No Caleb, it is weighed against the righteousness and holiness of God. No one can do enough good deeds to pay for what they did to you." Jacob assured him.

He looked satisfied, but Caleb was very wise and intelligent and as he pondered this he asked, "If our bad actions are weighed against the goodness of God and he is perfect, then what hope does anyone have of being good enough to be forgiven?"

"We don't, none of us are perfect Caleb, remember the story of the two wolves. The bible says that everyone, misses the mark, and fails to reach perfection, except Jesus. That is why he came to save everyone who has ever lived, from their imperfection. He transforms us into a new creation, if we allow him, but we need to let him in. We need to follow him. The choice is ours" I replied.

"It is just like your vision." Caleb noted deep in thought.

"Yes, it is like my vision." I answered solemnly.

Caleb frowned as he lamented, "But first we have to trust him, and then follow him, but how can I? I can't trust him when he didn't protect me!"

I genuinely felt Caleb's struggle deep inside; I was always prone to empathy. I tried to reconcile this as I spoke honestly, "I know how difficult it is to trust, Caleb. I too share this with you. Trust for me is earned, not freely given. I can't explain why God does not defend the weak, but I do know he is just and that he is limited by his own laws and regulations.

There is the law of sowing and reaping. There is the law of action and reaction, and there is a law of choice and consequence. I wish it were not so, I wish we did not have a free will and everything was pure and good, like God, but it's not, at least not yet.

We must battle our own darkness within as well as be on guard against the wickedness in others. The Devil is not our only enemy Caleb; don't forget that. You will meet many people in our day who will blame all kinds of depravity on the Devil, he isn't that powerful. We are all capable of great evil in our own rite and we all can perform noble deeds. Don't ever go about blaming the gods for our fate. Free will is very powerful, Caleb."

I feared that words had failed me, and yet I had to try to save Caleb from, shame, hatred and unforgiveness. Bitterness could easily destroy him, if he let it.

Caleb asked, "How can we have peace and joy without security, without trust, without knowing God?"

"We can't, but there is light is inside of you Caleb. You must meditate daily and search within, you will find him, but you must seek him always. Love can heal all wounds and light makes the darkness give way, but we must embrace it, focus on the Light and let it consume us and heal us from within. You can find that security and healing you long for Caleb. Pursue it." I pleaded.

"I'll try Commander, but what if I can't find him, what if I look inside..." He paused and looked down as he finished, "... and there is only darkness?"

I lifted my sleeve and showed him my tattoo and translated it, "Caleb this tattoo is Latin, it in means, 'In thy light we see the light.'"

Caleb frowned and read it aloud, "In lumine tuo videbimus lumen. Isn't Lumen the name of your enemy?"

Jacob smiled, "Yes and no, the man you know as Lumen is the Devil, Satan, but he goes by many names. He loves to pervert the things of God, Caleb. He is the false light."

I added, "Satan, or Lumen can appear as an angel of light, but Christ is the Light of God Caleb. This is the one my tattoo refers too and often we don't find him, he reaches down and shines on you and God willing, through you."

I could tell that he longed for that healing and that touch from God, he needed it. I would pray for him.

We reached the base of the mountain. We sat by the river for over an hour and continued to speak. I told him, "Caleb sometimes the darkness is the first that we see, but rejoice in this, for facing it shows that you are not blind and as disturbing as it is don't ignore it, and then seek for the eternal knowledge within. God has placed eternity in our hearts and he promised if we seek and don't give up we will find him. If you fail to see him in you, then look up."

I confessed, "There are times when I too find it hard to hear the Savior within and he generously makes me aware of him in his creation. God is the all in all. Sense him in the stars and moon, in the rays of sunshine on your face. His presence can be felt from the flowers, and the trees, the mountains and in the stream. Our Creator's imprint is there, but he is not the wind or the flower, still he is reflected in them.

Other times as I sit and wait upon the Lord, I have a vision and other times a dream. He also speaks to me through the confirming voice of others that I know and trust, but be careful because if you seek for God, by focusing only on that which is outside of you, especially through the wisdom of others, then you will be led astray. The Eternal is in you and all around you Caleb and he will always confirm it with his word.

You are still a child on the road to becoming a man, and as a child you are closer to this eternal knowledge then those who allow themselves to become distracted by the worries of the world. I know what was done to you has changed you, still try to remember the child you once were, and experience your true essence, before your uncle hurt you."

Caleb answered solemnly, "I think that child died a long time ago."

I placed my arm around him and I reminded him, "Perhaps Caleb, but Jesus raised the dead. He can revive all that was good and pure in you too. He will make you whole again."

"I hope so commander." Caleb replied as he wiped the tears from his eyes.

Caleb added, "I have never heard God's voice commander, but I heard your voice ordering me to remember my training."

Jacob questioned, "When was that Caleb?"

Caleb answered, "In the cave, last night. I heard her voice in my head."

Jacob looked at me with a raised eyebrow and Caleb continued, "I have never seen the Savior commander, but you saved me and I will forever be thankful. You will always have my allegiance."

"Thank you Caleb and call me Catherine" I smiled.

"I need to run again, are you going to be okay?" I inquired.

He nodded and got up to walk away and then he turned toward me again and asked, "Commander, I mean, Catherine, why is Jacob always with you?"

"He is my guardian, my protector." I replied

He ran back to me and embraced me, "You were my protector, what am I going to do when you leave?"

Tears filled my eyes again as I promised, "We will assign two for you, and their sole responsibility will be to both protect you and prepare you, so that no man will ever overpower you again. There are good men and women out there Caleb. We will find them and they will keep the bad men away. I promise that they will protect you."

Caleb looked up at Jacob who was also crying and asked, "Can I have them as big and as strong as Jacob? I like Jacob, I trust him. I can't say that of many people, except for a few, maybe Sayid and Sky and the Captain."

Jacob knelt down and he still towered over Caleb and said, "You are wise beyond your years Caleb, and we will try to find protectors like me for you."

Caleb smiled and embraced Jacob, "Thank you, thank you both. Would it be okay if I ran up the mountain again?"

I patted Jacob's back and said, "If you think you can keep up."

He beamed as he set off and said, "No problem." He needed our presence, our protection, and our love, and his company melted some of the resentment from my heart. Vengeance was not enough to give me peace, but Caleb's smile could.

I laughed as we chased him up the mountain, pacing ourselves most of the way until the last half where we easily passed him.

He thanked us when he got to the top, "Thanks for pretending to let me beat you for a while, but remember I've seen you two run before."

Jacob ruffled his hair and said, "You did very well Caleb."

"It's lunch time, let's go eat. I'm famished." I suggested and we all jogged down the well worn path.

We joined the others and Caleb never left our side. His little sister Sarah naturally attached herself to us as well.

She said nothing; she simply followed us around reaching up to take my hand on occasion, but usually she held close to her brother's side and he often placed a protective arm about her.

****

I sent Jacob to request from God directly to send forth two mighty warriors to protect them. It was not long before Jacob came and joined us by the fire one evening, with two massive men at his side. One looked like an older version of Caleb, he had long brown hair that hung freely about his shoulders and soft amber eyes, the other was a tall and lean. He was a muscular black male with dark brown eyes tinted with orange...

Jacob cleared his throat and said, "Caleb, Sarah, I would like you to meet your personal guardians. This is Karael and Uzziel."

Karael bowed and then shook Caleb's hand and said, "It is a pleasure to serve you, Master Caleb."

Caleb shook his hand and noted, "Karael, you look like me, but much bigger. That is a very strange name you have."

"Yes it is, Master Caleb." He agreed and continued, "It means, 'Angel who has the power to ruin demons. It is unique."

"Wow, cool, are you actually able to do that, I mean do you have that power?"

"Yes, God willing." Karael replied.

Caleb looked a little skeptical, but he also wanted to believe.

He shrugged and turned his attention to Uzziel as Sarah added, "Uzziel is another name I have never heard of; what does it mean?"

Uzziel bowed low and answered, "My name means, 'Strength of God.' I confess I do not have such strength, but all I do have, I pledge to your service and protection."

Sarah got up and shook Uzziel's hand as she said, "Thank you, it is very nice to meet you Uzziel."

Caleb then ran and hugged Jacob and I and said, "Thank you for keeping your promise to me. Does this mean you are leaving soon?"

I nodded and held him tight as I replied, "Soon, but not yet Caleb. Trust me in this; I leave you both in very good hands."

He nodded and kissed my cheek and said, "How can I ever thank you?"

Our little Caleb had to grow up too quickly, but I caressed his cheek for he was still a boy.

I replied, "Learn from these two all that you can, for a day will come when you must protect the weak. Strive to be a man of peace, but you must be prepared for the day of war. Today you begin a new life, Caleb in security and safety.

Don't be chained by your past Caleb. It is not what others do to you that define you; it is what you choose to do and who you chose to become. Be free, grow strong, and become a good man and you will be a warrior of God."

"I will, I love you Catherine." Caleb blushed. I kissed his cheek and assured him, "I love you too Caleb."

Caleb looked at his guardians and then back to me and whispered, "Are these two warriors of God?"

I smiled and whispered back, "Yes they are and they will not only protect you, they will train you. Now go show them your quarters. They will be by your side always, until the day when you release them from their duty." Caleb nodded and walked off with his faithful guardians at his side.

Peter leaned in and asked, "Don't you think that was a hell of a lot to put on the boys shoulders?"

"No" I replied, "He will have something to focus on other than his past and I already know who he will become."

"How?" Peter inquired skeptically

I smiled, "Remember what I told you about the vision I had on the mountain, with the two wolves."

"Yes." He answered.

"Well, what I failed to include was that I saw Caleb, Karael, Uzziel and his sister Sarah. They were much older than now and they were all standing in beautiful shiny armor, smiling in the distance." I explained as I noted Peter's disbelief and continued, "Don't worry love; I know that you don't believe in visions and dreams, but I do and I know Caleb will fulfill his destiny."

"How did you know it was Caleb in your vision and not another man and why didn't you tell him this before?" Peter probed.

I calmly responded, "I initially just sensed it was Caleb and I recognized his eyes, but it was not until I met Karael and Uzziel that I knew for sure. I didn't tell Caleb because I sensed that if I told him now he would choose another path in defiance against God, but I told Sarah. I made her promise not to tell Caleb until a day comes when Caleb is much older, when he is a man and he has doubts about his calling. I told her that it would be in a day before a great battle. I will also tell Karael, lest Sarah forget."

Peter sighed and ran his fingers through his hair and I added, "You don't approve? You would have me remain silent and let them choose their own fate without any direction from above?"

Peter looked into my eyes intensely as he spoke, "I would, hell Catherine, you place a lot of pressure on people with your dreams, visions, premonitions, and fucking messages from on high. If God has a message for Caleb or any of us, why the hell doesn't he tell us himself? I'm sorry, but it pisses me off."

I gently placed my hand on his and I felt the tension begin to melt away instantly as I answered, "I don't Peter, but I believe that Caleb will be okay and that my vision is a glimpse into the future. Whether it is in this world or the next, the spiritual realm or our own, I know not, but it is from God."

Peter squeezed my hand and got up to go for a walk in the darkness and ponder his convictions and struggle with his conflicting emotions, probably his love for me and his issues with my faith.

I will always pray Caleb will find healing, and find God. As I watched Caleb walk away in the far distance, with his guardians by his side, and Peter walking off in the opposite direction, I sighed. I was confident that the Caleb's defenders would help Caleb know the love and strength of God, and escape the pain, and bitterness of the past. Caleb was free to start anew and I knew that he would live up to his name. He too would become a warrior of God, but what of Peter? I could never see Peter's future and I hated not knowing. Peter's destiny was his own, but I will always pray that he finds God too.

*****

Chapter Two: New Life

Last night Peter saw me laughing while I sat by the fire and listened to the radio reporting that the dictator raged at the growing worldwide defiance. Peter found it a strange reaction and he flashed me an inquisitive look...

I spoke with laughter in my tone, "You see Peter; I used to resent mankind's free will. I was angry with those like you who chose not to accept Jesus as Savior and then I would weep for their choice, but God is so awesome and he has a sense of humor too. You see he is using rational people like you to cause the Devil grief. They refuse to believe in him, or serve him. Free will, who knew? God is good."

I could not help but laugh out loud and then I continued, "It's awesome, Satan wants to control man, but man's free will is so exquisite, those who stubbornly rejected the Lord also are equally defiant and refuse to submit to Lumen. It's so perfect, so beautiful. Who could have foreseen this?" I clapped my hands together.

I was sure that Peter did not understand why I was so pleased and I was very sure he must think me mad, but I could not contain myself. I knew he was still drawn toward me.

We were in high spirits that night and it had been a long time since we could all laugh together.

Laughter is contagious for even Jacob chuckled occasionally. I don't even recall what we were laughing at, regardless we could not stop and amidst this spectacle, Eric returned to camp.

Jason saw Eric first. He ran and embraced Eric for some time. He could not hold back his tears. Eric gently wiped the tears from his face and kissed him and Jason declared, "I am so glad you're okay. I had lost all hope that you would ever return. I feared I'd lost you."

Eric replied, "I was arrested, while I was in San Francisco."

We acknowledged Eric's presence and one by one embraced him and then a silence fell as we noticed that the back of his hand was severely damaged.

He hugged Peter and Sayid and then Eric kissed me saying, "Better to enter heaven without part of my hand then lose my soul, eh?"

I laughed as I embraced Eric. This time Peter did not share our laughter. He looked at us as if we were all crazy.

We sat and reminisced of days gone by. So much had changed and yet nothing had.

Peter asked Eric, "How did you escape?" Eric told us a remarkable story.

Eric began, "I was in the city after meeting with some underground computer techs there; I had known many of them from childhood. We were so careful and we thought that we could successfully meet in secret at the university library, but the government stormed the facility and arrested all of us.

We were imprisoned in a large storage facility as we awaited our trials. There were hundreds of us being detained and the evidence was heavily weighted in the prosecution's favor, even though it was all circumstantial. The government is rounding up all known computer hackers in the country. We were all incarcerated with no hope for escape."

Peter had a slight grimace on his face, barely detectable by anyone else, but I noticed. Peter could not get past the fact that God didn't protect me, nor could he forgive himself, feeling it was his testimony that helped condemn me to the insane asylum, where government soldiers raped me. I didn't blame Peter, but I knew he still blamed himself, as well as my God.

Peter helped me escape and next to Jacob and Sayid, who are bound to me by duty, Peter is the only one who has ever protected me. I could never blame him, but I didn't know how to stop him from blaming himself for what happened to me.

I turned my attention back to Eric as he continued, "They found my lap top and on it where various hacking programs and I was in possession of several illegal technologies, and applications, some of which were from the factories we destroyed in our operations together. I was found guilty of conspiracy, treason and murder. They sentenced me to be electrocuted on TV for the entire world to see.

I had time to pray and I did not fear death. The Lord had set me free long ago and how I longed to see his face.

I was asked if I had any last words and I was compelled to say, 'My God is able to deliver me from your power, for He alone is the one and only true God, but if He desires to deliver me into your hand, then so be it. God's will be done.'

At this moment they pulled the switch. Electricity shot through my body, but I felt no pain, I died. All was black and silent. I could see past the veil of this life, but before I could cross over I was jolted back to life. Lightning flowed from my fingertips, as if through a conductor and it killed my executioner, as well as the guards who bound me.

They cut the power and left me restrained in the chair. I did not understand fully what had happened; still I knew God had stayed their power over me. I glorified His name."

"O God is so awesome. Praise the Lord." I could not contain my praise, so of course I didn't try.

Peter looked skeptical. He could not believe his ears. He then motioned and asked Eric, "What happened to your hand."

Eric smiled and said, "They assumed they couldn't kill me, I think they knew it was God whom had saved me. So, while I was restrained they put a chip in my hand.

That night I realized the Lord had allowed this electricity to fill me. I prayed and my cell door opened and I walked into the hall. There were two guards at the very end of the hall conversing with one another, but they didn't see me.

There was a guard at the other end of the hall standing watching me and looking at the monitors and back to me, but he said nothing; he just kept watching as I approached him. No one had seen me save this one guard. He was a genetically engineered soldier who had a number designation, but there was no name on his uniform.

I asked him, "Are you going to let me pass?" He gazed at me with a touch of admiration in his eyes as he replied, "Perhaps.".

I smiled up at him and asked him, "What's your name?"

He replied with a raised eyebrow, "My name, I don't have a name. I am Servant 678."

I inquired, "Doesn't it brother you to be dehumanized like that?"

He pondered and replied, "They say that I am not human. I am engineered and grown in a lab."

"Do you have feelings, emotions, private thoughts, and dreams?" I asked with all sincerity.

He, smiled and said, "Yes, but I have never shared them, except with my closest," He paused searching for the appropriate word, "...friends. They say that I am an abomination."

"Yeah well, they've said that about me too, but God doesn't make mistakes, so how can you not be human?" I replied.

"Apparently, I do not have a soul." He declared coldly.

"Do you love?" I asked

"I have never known love. I care deeply for my friends, but I care nothing for most people."

"Hmm" I sighed, "Well that's true for many people, so I believe you have a soul."

"He smiled slightly and I asked him again, "Are you going to let me pass?"

He stepped aside and replied, "You may go, but I sense I probably could not stop you if I tried. I saw the attempted execution. No one opened the doors for your cell, yet here you are. No one has even seen you in the corridor. I have been watching the cameras on the security feed as you came down the hall every camera that you walk past stops recording. The picture is like snow on the screen. It is as if there is some kind of electronic interference. This must be the hand of your God."

"He's not just my God; He is God, Lord of all." I replied.

Then the guard noticed my hand and he said, "They will track you. You will not get far."

"True, do you have a knife?" I inquired. Servant 678 warned, "You cannot cut it out, it will cause a tracking alarm to go off in a few seconds and they will order a lock down. You will never get out."

"I have seven seconds to place it in living flesh before it does." I continued, "Perhaps you could act as my recipient and then later you can remove it; you heal very quickly don't you?"

He contemplated what I said and then he replied, "Yes, but if I am suspected they will kill me, so why would I help you?"

"Because you're helping me now by letting me leave." I smiled.

"This is true. I will do as you ask." He then gave me a bowie knife strapped to his ankle. We made our way to a bathroom behind the security desk.

I cut the chip from the back of my hand and then I apologized as he rolled up his pant leg. I cut a slit in his calf and I slipped the microchip in the flap of his skin.

Then he assured me, "I will stay in the bathroom for ten minutes and then I will flush the chip down the toilet. That is as long as I can wait, or they will know I helped you."

"Thank you, I'm eternally grateful." I said with all sincerity.

He ordered, "Go before the other guards return to start their rounds. You have fifteen minutes."

"I thought you were giving me ten." I smiled.

"I am being generous, but they will begin their rounds in fourteen minutes, so get going. " I nodded and I left him.

I walked passed his security desk and said over my shoulder as I ran backwards for a few steps facing him, "Thank you and you really should get yourself a name. Maybe Vincent, you look like a Vincent"

He smiled and I waved goodbye as every door was open before me, not a single one was locked. I walked out of the prison unnoticed and then I heard the alarms.

I set off and sought President Davidson, who was at my execution and had witnessed all that had happened to me."

Jason said with a twinge of jealousy mixed with teasing, "It was probably your smile that enticed that engineered soldier to let you go."

Eric placed his arm around Jason and laughed, "Well, then be thankful he did and praise God he gave me such a gorgeous smile." Jason shook his head and could not help but smile too and then we all laughed, save Peter.

Peter looked suspicious as he noted, "They let you go Eric. They let you escape. It was too easy. Could they have planted another tracking device on you that you don't know about?"

"I thought the same thing, I checked myself thoroughly. I'm clean." Eric assured us and then he said, "Time's short, Catherine I must speak to you and Peter in private."

He got up led us toward the river, a safe distance away to converse with Peter and I alone. Eric had a message from the president to Peter informing us that Augustus' forces were closing in on our location. Eric had almost completed the design of a virus to destroy the enemy's computer communication systems. He was also busy working on regaining control of our perimeter defense system. It was close to completion, but the president said that I had to be made safe. Eric said, "Davidson said that was his first priority."

I did not trust the president and I was proud of Peter when he asked, "Why is he concerned about her safety?"

Eric answered cautiously, "He has received intelligence about the child inside you." Eric paused and gaged my reaction; I was not very good at hiding my feelings.

I know suspicion was evident, still he continued, "Augustus had large numbers of soldiers who were genetically enhanced through injections, but their life expectancy is diminished by developing an aggressive form of cancer that attacks their lymphatic system.

He has found a way to grow them in a lab. The soldiers are formed in a Petri dish and engineered to be physically perfect and free from the anomaly; however they age far too quickly. They age at such a rapid rate that their adult life is only estimated to be ten to fifteen years.

The president believes that you, Jacob, and your child Catherine, hold the key to defeating him."

"Our DNA..." I sighed. "...why does everyone think I'm genetically enhanced?"

Peter replied, "Because it is the only logical explanation to explain how you can do all that you are capable of. Catherine, you should not be able to defeat me, nor exceptionally trained men like Sayid, let alone others who have been genetically enhanced. His interest in Jacob and your child are obvious."

"I suppose your right Peter, but I'll never let any of them get their hands on my child."

Eric nodded in reply and added, "The president is convinced that you are a warrior of God, but he still suspects that your DNA differs from the rest of us.

I don't know how he plans to get a hold of you, but I suspect it is part of his plan in bringing you to a safe location."

Peter remarked, "I think you're right Eric. How large a fighting force does the enemy have? How long does it take for them to become adult?"

"Unknown." Eric replied and then he added, "I suspect it's very rapid. I think I can find out exactly how long, Servant 678 is one of them; I could hack in and try to download the appropriate files before we take down the system in the attack."

I inquired, "How does knowing Servant 678 is one of them help you?"

Eric grinned, "It enables me to narrow my search parameters when I go fishing. Do you really want to know the technical details?"

I smiled and replied, "No."

Then Peter asked Eric "Does the President know we have the ability to inject our own soldiers with the Super Soldier serum?"

Eric replied, "No, He isn't aware that Yuri ever gave us the vials. Did Sky succeed in replicating them?"

"Yes, however now that we know they are likely to give our men cancer, I'm glad we didn't use them. Sky must fix the anomaly. If only we had 678's DNA." I responded with relief.

Eric continued, "We do. I have the knife I cut him with, but my DNA is on it too. I kept the knife in case I needed it in my escape."

Eric takes the knife from his back pack and gives it to me. I was very pleased as I said, "Keep it. After our meeting, bring this to Sky and tell him what it is. You're amazing Eric."

"Thanks Cat. If I can find out where Servant 678 resides, I believe he will help me get in and accomplish my mission for the president. It would make our job a lot easier if we had someone on the inside to get me in, as well as implement our plan for our offensive.
We've already had to postpone our attack three times due to my arrest and logistical issues, but the final date approaches quickly. Yuri has told me that the other leaders say it's still a go; none of them have been captured.

Our plan is perfect; it'll succeed, but if I can get Servant 678's cooperation, then there is nothing Augustus or Lumen can do to stop us. Still you must be made safe, Cat. Everyone is hunting you." Eric said as he gave me a locator beacon as he continued, "It's from Davidson. He said that a chopper will come and fly you to a secure location."

I sighed, "I know I have to flee, but I don't trust Davidson. Peter, you know the president better than all of us, what do you think?"

He replied honestly. "There is no doubt that Davidson wants to rule all of North America, but I believe he really does love America and he would do everything in his power to protect her.

Whether he cares about you, your child, or any of the rebels, I don't know. He may use you as pawns, or he may really believe you are some divinely equipped leader sent by God to help humanity in this war. He could also be playing both sides. I don't know Catherine, but I certainly don't trust him either.

If we activate this beacon it could be a trap. I also think he would try to take your child, if it holds the key to ultimate victory."

I nodded in agreement and Peter continued, "Regardless, I believe Eric should return and proceed with our attack on schedule, as well as aid in the president's plan to protect America. As for Servant 678, I believe it's too risky to include him in this phase of the attack, but after the mission is a success we should see if we can turn him."

I agreed, "We will continue as planned and use Yuri's men to dress as Augustus' soldiers.

Eric can attempt to recruit 678 and Sky will search for a cure for both models of super soldiers. Maybe they can be turned if we can promise them long life."

I looked to Eric and ordered, "Proceed. Don't include the president in any of our plans. Now, go find Sky and brief him. It's likely that Augustus and Satan won't pour any resources, or energy into saving those already sick, but we will administer a cure for those who dare to trust us."

Peter said, "Catherine you heal at a rate far greater than any of us, perhaps you should give Sky a few vials of your blood before we leave, it may help him find a cure more quickly, especially to slow the aging process."

I sighed, "Fine, but only Sky is allowed access to it. Not the president, not anyone."

Eric nodded, even though he had been working with the president's men to regain control the perimeter defense system, I knew I could trust him and the perimeter defense was the only thing protecting North America from nuclear attack. He told us that he was working as fast as he could for President Davidson, who feared an attack was imminent.

Eric assured me, "Cat, Davidson asked me to assure you that you won't have to worry. You and your child are going to a safe place. Even if our enemies attack, you'll be safe. A stealth helicopter will come once we activate the beacon."

"Eric, we will be activating it, but I'll have Sayid fly her to a destination of our choosing. You can have one of the guides lead the President's pilot to him by foot." Peter replied.

I added, "Sayid will continue to lead our rebel forces, so go and brief him as well, but bring your knife to Sky first." Eric nodded

Eric hugged us; I know he did not want to say good–bye so quickly. He was such a gentle loving soul. I was glad he was free, but it saddened me that he lost part of his hand.

Peter added, "Eric I also would like you to tell Davidson, that Catherine lost the child. Tell him that she's no longer pregnant."

"I will Captain. Commander, God bless you both." Eric turned and walked away.

Jacob spoke, "You impress me Peter Joseph Roberts."

Peter raised an eyebrow and inquired, "How did I manage to do that?"

Jacob replied, "Even though I do not condone deception, you are wise."

Peter grinned, "Well I don't know about that, but thank you Jacob." Then Peter frowned as he continued, "I am troubled that Davidson knows that you where impregnated. If this was Augustus's doing, how did he have knowledge of it?"

I was perplexed too as I answered, "I don't know, but I am thankful for your insight. It is good to make Davidson believe that there is no child for him to try and get his clutches into. You are a very cunning, my love."

"Well I was hoping you weren't keeping me around for just my looks." Peter smiled.

I laughed, "Actually I was, the brains are just a bonus."

Peter kissed me and smiled, "I'll go order the camp to pack-up quickly for immediate dispersal." I nodded and then he went to prepare for the departure.

*****

Sayid was pleased that he would accompany us. He knew that we would need a pilot, and he was able to operate every kind of military craft. After he flew us to our location he would rejoin the others to launch our offensive; I knew that he would be more effective knowing that I was safe.

We activated the beacon after the camp dispersed. A stealth helicopter soon arrived. Sayid aimed a gun at the pilot's head once we were on board. He said, "Forgive me, but there has been a slight change in plans. Please turn off the chopper and get out." The pilot complied.

Peter ordered, "Eric, disable the tracking system, this is undoubtedly low-jacked."

Eric did not take long and while he worked on the helicopter I walked to the edge of the forest as Peter and Sayid loaded the chopper with survival gear, while I stared at a lone white wolf who was watching me intently.

I got down on one knee. The wolf walked up to me and allowed me to pet him. I asked the wolf, "Will you take this and run with it all day and all night and drop it wherever you desire?" I opened my palm and the wolf appeared to nod and I pet him again. He then took the positioning sensor and the locator beacon in his mouth and ran off.

I noticed that Peter had been watching me the whole time. He could not believe his eyes and when I approached he said sarcastically, "What, are you able to communicate with wild animals too?"

I just smiled and declared, "Time to leave."

Peter gave Sayid the coordinates to one of the president's hideouts.

Sayid said, "We will fly toward the east for a while so the pilot on the ground doesn't know our direction."

Sayid then headed deep into the Rocky Mountains to a private house built right in the rocks. This may have been where the president had planned on hiding me all along, but he would not guess we would use his chopper to fly there anyways.

It could never be seen if you didn't know where it was. It was massive. Sayid hovered while we descended from the chopper onto the mountain top and we all waved good-bye as he flew away.

*****

Peter, Jacob and I lived well for we had a large amount of supplies. The time of my son's birth was at hand, I was only seven months pregnant when I went into labor.

I screamed in agony as I brought the child into the world. It was the worst torture I had ever experienced in my life. I thought that I would die from the pain, but after he was born it was as if all my pain was forgotten. In an instant joy and peace filled my spirit. I gave birth on February 8th.

Peter asked me, "What are you going to name him?"

I paused and then I kissed his forehead as I replied, "John Raziel."

Peter looked at me with a little bit of surprise and he inquired, "That's a unique name, why did you choose it?"

I smiled as I said, "Yes it is, a unique name for a unique child."

Jacob noted, "It is a very good name; John is a Hebrew name that means beloved gift of the Lord and Raziel means Secret of Jehovah, or God's secret."

Jacob approved as he said, "That is a very good choice Catherine."

I replied honestly, "It was God's choice."

It was such a relief to be myself again, with no military or religious responsibilities. I felt myself enjoying the spiritual silence that I had recently. I had not encountered the demonic for almost a year. I had not encountered God lately either, until he spoke into my spiritual ear, when Peter asked what the baby's name was to be. God answered inside my mind, "John Raziel." I felt a sense normalcy again.

My child gave me new life. My vibrant nature returned. I was the happiest I had ever been. I loved my son, I loved Peter and he loved me.

I cherished our seclusion from the world, but we could not ignore it completely. The hideaway had a satellite radio and a television and Internet; I guess it was designed as a command center or out post should Russia attack. We listened to the news, but not often.

China was growing increasingly aggressive and actively resisted the limitations on their powers by the New World Order. They also publicly opposed being involved in the North American and Russian Alliance.

I was thankful we had secure internet that enabled us to communicate with Eric as well as rebel leaders across the globe.

Our British and Canadian allies informed us that Russia was playing both sides and Yuri confirmed this Intel for us. His nation like many was divided; political forces on one side and the military split in their allegiance, but the rebel leaders in the resistance remained loyal to us. Yuri had the navy backing him and some of the air force, but the ground troops supported the politicians.

The official Russian government leaders, the politicians, were secretly negotiating with China and after a terrorist attack on France; England had to be more diplomatic in their dealings with China as well.

Nations were crumbling from within as chaos threatened to erupt in nations around the globe. With politicians and their armies on one side and the rebels on the other, all Augustus had to do was exert enough pressure to cause civil unrest and inspire civil wars.

He was a master manipulator and tactician, as was the Devil himself. They were hoping the nations would focus on destroying themselves and the World Government would simply move in and restore peace.

The dictator's grip had weekend in the past year and few humans embraced the self-proclaimed deity Lumen as God. This gave us hope in humanity again as America pursued liberty. America was growing stronger as one North American power base, but The Middle Eastern Nations began to fall apart.

True Muslims waged jihad against the dictator Augustus and his false god, who was failing to keep his hold over mankind. The Middle East was in utter chaos and mankind became more resistant to their loss of free will.

The micro-chipping process had failed since rebel groups had destroyed the manufactures at every turn across the globe.

All around the world people had resorted to a barter system of trade again; they no longer used microchip cards obtained on the black market.

I continued to focus on my child for the next few months and then one day we saw from our mountain home the missals shooting above us. The radio was on and we heard the announcer saying, "America is under attack… This just in, a series of bombs have detonated outside the perimeter defense system in both the Atlantic and Pacific Oceans.

Huge tilde waves are making their way toward America's Coastal Communities. There is no stopping it. Surely Millions will die. North Korea claimed responsibility for an attack from the south while Russia is attacking from the north."

I knew the perimeter defense system was running and it had detected and destroyed most of the weapons before they hit the ground. I was happy Eric succeeded in regaining control of that system; still, the enemy had a contingency plan. They deliberately detonated dirty bombs all along America's coastlines outside the perimeter defense system. The nuclear cloud would have surely thrown us into nuclear winter.

I gave my son to Peter to hold, as I was filled with the Spirit and I walked out on to a natural stone balcony that overlooked the mountains. I lifted my hands and I prayed in a language I had never known.

I said, "Abwûn, Nehwê tzevjânach aikâna d'bwaschmâja af b'arha. Ela patzân min bischa. Metol dilachie malkutha wahaila wateschbuchta l'ahlâm almîn.Adon Olam, attæm rg gr oyēb rwnb æl lsl Ze rah har qz"x' māzāq liyax µayil veata axUr rûaµ yiK kî Pi. K ken lfxfn nāµāl wadi &n nś rUs sûr Q., Hi. ata reb ebær Boker fnf ānān Amên."

Peter watched on mesmerized as I uttered these words. He did not understand the tongue in which I had spoken, as I stood on the balcony with my arms in the air praying to the Living God.

I was overlooking all the mountains below us. We lived in a home carved out of the mountain and my words passed through earth and sky. As I spoke my voice echoed through the mountain chain like a rolling thunder. My arms reached toward the heavens and the winds swirled about me. I continued my prayer in a long forgotten language, as a great vortex rose from the mountains. My hair ripped about, but my body could not be dislodged. The power of the winds I summoned was so great that I momentarily feared that Peter would lose hold of John, my son. I glanced back and saw that Jacob held onto both of Peter and my baby. I turned back toward the mountains and continued praying.

"What language is she speaking?" Peter asked Jacob as the winds gained strength swirling all around the room.

Jacob shouted, "She speaks in the language of the Master, her Lord."

He listened as Jacob translated my prayer, "Catherine prays, ' Oh Thou, from whom the breath of life comes, let your will come true , in the universe just as on earth, but let us be freed from that what keeps us off from our true purpose. From you becomes evident the all-working force, the lively strength to act, and the song that beautifies all and restores itself from age to age. Master of the earth, drive out our enemy's fire towards the sea, this mountain strong power, Wind Spirit therefore bring an end to this. Rush forward, carry, and remove it from the region beyond in a cloud. Sealed in trust, faith and truth, I confirm with my entire being. So be it.' She spoke forth the word of God"

Peter did not know what to make of it, but I was moved to turn up the radio where the announcer informed us that, a mighty wind swept across all of North America in a giant swirl as several tornados formed and it propelled the funnel clouds across the ocean to the west, toward the north and toward the south.

Peter could not believe what he heard, or what he witnessed. The winds subsided shortly after I had come back in from the balcony. Peter said nothing; he was perplexed.

As the winds near us subsided, I went and turned off the radio and turned on the television. We watched huge waves forming and coming toward the coast of California. From the angle of the cameras it looked like a wall of white water moving forward at a tremendous speed. These were the largest waves I had ever seen.

Peter stated, "That Tsunami will surely result in the death of millions of innocent people." Then suddenly the winds picked up and the giant wave looked as if it hit a giant invisible wall of energy and then it dissipated into nothingness.

Peter's rational explanations escaped him. He said, "What just happened?"

I smiled and knelt before him. Jacob took John as I prayed for Peter. I gently said in that same foreign tongue, "Ef-teh ayouneck"

Peter asked Jacob, "What does that mean?"

Jacob replied, "Open your eyes"

Peter watched the television with us as hundreds of men, dressed in white robes, were on TV. They were standing in the water with their hands in the air. They stood all along the coastline and they spoke the same language that I had just uttered. The men on TV had a light shining about them and that same light was shining about Jacob and I.

I told Peter, "The angels are calming the sea." Peter did not yet know by whose power this occurred, but surely he could no longer deny that some strange force did command the winds and the seas. I hoped that he could see that I could ask God and had the ability with his word summon this power?

I told him, "Peter, God's power is limitless; we ask and we receive. Nothing is too hard for him. If it is his will, then no power on earth or in the heavens can stop him. He usually allows us to suffer the horrible consequences of our decisions, but praise be to God, he gives us the power of intercession. We have power in his name."

I praised God for opening Peter's eyes and then I said, "Peter My Love, how does it feel to be given sight." He made no reply.

He held me close, enveloping me in his embrace. There was no better place. He did not know how to reply, so I said nothing as he kissed my face.

Jacob said, "Well little brother now that you can see you must seek." He said this as he placed a bible in Peter's hand.

For the first time in my life with Peter he read the bible, while trying to be more open and he delved into the Word of God with such veraciousness and a single-minded purpose to discover the truth, but the more he read it the more agitated he became.

I know he read it before when he was young. He told me that God seemed cruel. Last year he asked, "Why would a creator create humanity with such a weak human nature and then blame them for their weakness? It is madness to me."

He could no longer deny a higher power existed, but the Hebrew God seemed too punishing and to petty for him to accept.

Peter scoffed, "Do you really believe God created the heavens and the earth in seven days. It is nonsense and how can you have evening and morning on each day when the sun and the moon does not yet exist. It is nonsense. You would have to completely ignore science and dismiss all rational thought to believe such ridiculous claims."

"Actually Peter the big bang theory and intelligent design are not that far apart from each other, the order of creation is almost identical. The original Hebrew describes creation quite differently from the poor English translation of it." I assured him.

"How?" Peter retorted with a slight agitation in his voice.

Jacob informed him," The original ancient Aramaic and Hebrew is better translated, 'There was chaos and order in the first era.' It is poorly translated by most bibles as, 'There was morning and evening on the first day.'

Jacob continued, "Furthermore instead of, God said, 'Let there be light.' It would be more accurate to say, 'Let there be energy, and there was energy.'

Peter shook his head and asked, "Then why doesn't the English translation say that?"

"Man is notorious for misquoting God and misunderstanding the point of his word." Jacob stated as a matter of fact.

I added, "Peter the point is that God is the creator, He is one, Elohim, father, spirit, son, all present and involved in creation. He wants us to be one with him and He alone brings order to our chaos, both in creation and in us."

I don't think my words helped, still, Peter kept reading and tried to keep an open mind. Then one day as he was reading, he suddenly he seemed overwhelmed and he threw the book down saying, " I don't see you, I don't hear you and I sure as hell don't trust you!"

I sat beside Peter and I suggested, "Peter, forget about the Old Testament for now. Read John and then the other three gospels, then we will talk and go on from there."

He nodded, but in my heart I knew that he firmly believed that the Hebrew God could not be God. I asked, "What made you so angry?"

"I was reading when Joshua fought and god made the sun stand still. That is impossible Catherine." Peter said with frustration.

Jacob informed Peter, "I know you may not believe this Peter, but on the other side of the earth at this time, there were a people who had the legend of the longest night. You can research it in the Mexican Annals of Cuauhtitlan. Nothing is impossible for God. Time is in his hands."

I did not know what feelings would be evoked by his reading the New Testament, I knew he read it before as well, but at least he was willing to examine it again. Maybe he would be like Eric, a Red Letter Christian.

Eric did not cling to close to the Hebrew version of God either, but he did embrace the teachings and believed in Jesus Christ.

Peter read the entire New Testament. Peter, like Eric, did not embrace Paul's teachings either. Eric once labeled Paul a, 'Johnny come lately.' I never asked him what that meant, nor did I ever argue with him over his doctrinal beliefs, but I knew I loved him and I knew he was one of the most loving men I had ever known, next to Brother John.

I smiled remembering Brother John for a moment. I had not seen him since I got on the plane to leave Ireland, but I missed him. I said a brief prayer for him and then my thoughts returned to Peter.

Peter told me that he thought that the Hebrew God appeared to be a different God then the one

Jesus proclaimed. I could not blame him for this point of view. Had God not revealed himself to me, I would probably share that view too.

Peter finished the New Testament and he said, "Jesus taught love, forgiveness kindness, and mercy. He ordered his followers to not judge, to love and even be pacifistic.

The New Testament God was very different from the legalistic, jealous, angry god of the Hebrews that punished disobedience with wrath and vengeance. He accepted an eye for and eye, but Jesus preached turn the other cheek and forgive, returning evil with good. I can't follow either version of God!"

Peter sighed, "I am sorry Catherine, but I'm a soldier. I admired the peaceful pacifist of Jesus, as much as I admire historical figures like Gandhi, Siddhartha, Confucius and the Dahlia Lama. All of these men are noble and admirable, but I am not a pacifist. I could never follow a religious leader that preaches turn the other cheek.

I don't want war, but you know that sometimes it is necessary and if anyone hit me, you know I would hit him back. I don't know how you, or Sayid, and Jacob reconcile these two versions of God, or how you follow the peaceful Jesus when we all must kill as soldiers."

Peter could not understand, but I tried my best to explain, "Jesus does preach love, forgiveness, and turn the other cheek; this is true. You know I am not very good at following his path of righteousness, but I do love and I take his command to us, to never judge, to heart..." I paused and then continued, "... with the exceptions of rapists and pedophiles of course."

I shrugged my shoulders and professed, "I truly believe that we are all made in the image and likeness of God, therefore we must respect and honor everyone we meet. I don't always succeed in living this out, but I try.

I believe that Jesus is the perfect example of what we should aspire to, but it is not being a good follower that saves me, it is the trust and faith I have in the belief that he is the son of God who died for me and paid for every sin that I have committed and every sin that I will commit in the future.

He paid for it all on the cross and he died and rose again. He lives and he lives in me, helping me become all that I was designed by my creator to be, no matter what that is. He helps me to endeavor and to excel.

Furthermore Jesus is the, 'Prince of Peace' the first time he came to save us and shower us with mercy and grace, but soon he returns as a warrior king Peter, the King of kings. He is not a pacifist.

The bible tells us, 'In as much as it does depend on you, live at peace with one another.' He wants us to embrace peace, but when war is waged against us we fight back, some of us fight on our knees and others with our hands."

"Isn't that a contradiction and hypocritical? 'He who lives by the sword, dies, by the sword, return evil with good, pray for your enemies.' These are his teachings and a soldier cannot live by this code. Except the sword part, a combatant knows this to be likely. You cannot follow Jesus and wage war against your fellow man Catherine." Peter was earnest, yet I sensed that he did not want to call me a hypocrite; he was just trying to make sense of it all.

I searched for the words to convince him as I declared, "Peter look at us. We in our nature long for peace and would choose peace over war, however we are simultaneously warriors who must fight for justice and against oppression. This in a small way reflects the image of God.

We are all in need of saving Peter, and we cannot achieve our best without God in our lives. We need him; I need him to help me be a leader, a warrior, a mother, and one day a wife."

Peter could not help, but smile when I said wife and then he said seriously, "I know what you believe Catherine, I just don't know if Jesus is really the son of God and it makes no rational sense that he would even have to pay the price for everyone's sin.

Any God who is supposed to be all knowing, and our creator, who is love would not create children only to see them condemned save the small number who believe in his son.

Furthermore the bible also says in the Old Testament and Jesus repeated it in the New Testament that we would be judged according to our deeds, those who commit evil will rise to be condemned and those who do good will rise to live again. So if we are judged by our actions then why does everyone need a savior?"

I could not make Peter believe, I knew that, only God could, but I had to try so I said, "Peter you are correct that humans are judged by our deeds, and Jesus is the judge and our defense.

A Christian is a part of the kingdom of God and all who accept him receive the rights, and privileges that come with receiving Christ as Savior, as Lord and King. It enables us to be counseled and strengthened by his Spirit, it enables us to have power in his name, to intercede through prayer and talk with God the Father anytime, anyplace and anywhere and it grants us entrance to eternal life, because we are forgiven."

Peter rolled his eyes and said, "A get out of Jail free card. Tell me, why do we not hear him talking back? Why doesn't he answer our prayers, auditable, not in your heart or in your spirit, but for real?"

"He does answer prayer Peter, You just witnessed that. If you heard his voice or saw him face to face, you would presume you were hallucinating anyways. You would think yourself mad and not trust your senses. You are the ultimate rationalist Peter and that is okay, but it does make faith a difficult step to take." I sighed.

Peter interjected, "Exactly Catherine, why are answered prayers, miracles and encounters with God private, personal. They are never witnessed by everyone, they are never scientifically measurable. Why doesn't he perform mass miracles like recorded in the bible for everyone to see?

Look how many prayers go unanswered, people all over the world pray and die of disease and disaster anyways. Jesus said ask and you shall receive, not might or maybe."

I informed him, "Prayer is not like going to the candy store or gift shop and receiving whatever you request. It is more like approaching your Father the King and in his wisdom he grants or denies that request. We trust his will be done in our lives. Furthermore chaos remains; it is still a real force, in nature, in the universe, and in us."

Peter retorted, "Convenient."

I took a deep breath so that I didn't come across as exasperated and I continued, "There was once a song I sung in church as a child, based on the scriptures it went something like this, 'One day every knee will bow, one day every tongue will confess that you are Lord, but still the greatest treasure remains for those who gladly choose you now.' You see Peter Jesus will return one day and every eye will see him and know, but I as a part of his royal family have rights and privileges and power ordained by God."

Peter had a pain and resentment in his eyes tinged with rage as he said in a cold calm tone, "Well, those privileges, and power didn't protect you when you were incarcerated, did they?"

I touched his arm and said, "No it didn't, in this world Jesus warned us that we would face, trial, tribulation, attacks from evil men. Men can choose to do evil or be good; but Jesus did promise he would never leave us, we would endure and he heals, restores and renews. He alone makes all work good in the end. He just wants us to believe and trust that he will."

"I don't think I can do that when I can't even see, hear or touch him. Sorry Catherine, I just can't blindly believe." Peter said sincerely.

I kissed his lips and said, "I know you can't Peter, but you are well named. You are as immovable as rock and your rational side, it is impenetrable and that's okay, for God made you that way and I love you."

Jacob added, "Maybe you were supposed to be named Thomas."

I laughed, and reminded them, "Yes, but Jesus loved Thomas too and showed himself to Thomas. He wrote my favorite gospel. Jesus showed Thomas, he will do likewise for Peter, I just don't know when."

Peter question, "What gospel did Thomas write?"

Jacob responded, "All of the disciples wrote a gospel including Mary Magdalene. Power hungry men and sexist politicians tried to hide them from the faithful."

Peter asked, "Why aren't they included in the bible today?"

I sighed, "Politics and power Peter, there are fifty other gospels about Jesus."

Many gospels support Jesus as fully man, even married to Marry Magdalene."

Jesus treated women as equal before God; men did not want this to survive. They tried to continue the subjugation of woman and succeeded for centuries."

Jacob interjected, "Yes it is true, the society of men was warped and misguided. Jesus had loved Mary and women were the first to spread the good news. Male leadership regained dominance in the church shortly after Jesus left. Many viewed sex as evil, women as temptresses and blamed them for the failings of men rather than address their own darkness within, thus they ensured any writings that considered Jesus as fully man or women as equal where destroyed and their supporters killed, but he was both man and divine. He had to be to face temptation and win. God is greater than the futile plotting of men."

I added, "God protected the lost gospels and had them released to the academic world in December 1945. A Christmas gift from God was found in Egypt at Nag Hammadi. A library that was filled with many books from the early Christians was found there. The gospel of Thomas, was the most widely read among them. "

"So why do you revere this book so much if its writings where chosen for political and social reasons." Peter challenged.

I smiled, "Just because it is incomplete, does not mean truth is not to be found within its pages. Your understanding of Jesus is limited when you fail to read the other accounts of him, you'll have a limited perspective, but his wisdom and teachings are still there."

Peter informed me, "Well I am done reading that bible, and I didn't receive any answers just more questions Catherine. I will not be reading it again." Peter and I remained religiously divided, but our love for each other didn't diminish.

I kissed him and said, "That's okay Peter, God will reveal himself to you. He will save you when the time is right. I don't expect you to believe right now just because I do, but will you promise me one thing?"

I placed my hand on his arm and he said, "That depends on what it is."

I looked up and pleaded, "Just be open. When you witness something beyond reason, beyond your understanding and you see anything that is undeniably miraculous and God shows himself to you, please don't rationalize it. Don't ignore it, and don't assume you're crazy. Take a step of faith and dare to believe."

Peter bent down and kissed my forehead and then he replied, "I will look for a rational explanation, but I will try to be open to any experience good, or evil. I say show me and I will believe."

I gasped, "Peter don't say that, take it back. You don't know what you're saying. I have seen Satan and his demons and I can assure you that you do not want any experience with them, ever."

He replied, "Well, if I saw Satan himself then I would know God is real too. I would definitely choose the right side. Show me any proof, any at all. If God is here let me see him, if his son is our savior, why doesn't he appear? If Satan is real, then where is he? I'm sorry Catherine, but I must see to believe and even then you're right, I would probably require further proof."

I sighed, "I love you, but this is a futile discussion. I just pray it is God you encounter and not the enemy."

Peter put John back in my arms and he seemed oblivious to all that just had happened. Peter kissed me and we put the baby down to sleep and then we went to train…

*****

Eric later informed us of other details in the attack on North America. We were not the only targets. Eric discovered that Chinese missiles were launched, from a fleet in the Pacific and the Atlantic as well, while the Russians and Koreans attacked simultaneously. China used India and launch sights in Africa, in a simultaneous assault against the New World Order and in the anti-American offensive.

It was an all-out nuclear war and China was controlling all the players. Missiles had raged through the skies like the roaring thunder. The great Asian dragon breathed the fires across our North American skyline and throughout the sea. I praised God that he intervened.

The nations were in chaos and confusion, and Augustus tried to maintain their grip of power, while foolish politicians, played politics trying to win favor from the populace at home and not lose Augustus's support from abroad.

Eric said that the resistance was growing, but rebel leaders needed someone to give the people hope and direction, to inspire them. He wanted me to send him a video clip over the internet and he would release them to the people...

I complied, but I feared that I was not a very good public speaker, and then Yuri contacted me as well. He said, "Catherine, the people need to know that you are alive and believers have to see you too."

"Why me? Why don't you make the speech, or Yamomoto, or Sayid?" I retorted.

Yuri replied with a chuckle, 'Because dorogoy, we are not you. The people believe you are a warrior of God, and they need to believe this, for many fear they are waging war against the Devil himself. We also need you to inspire the Christians."

Yuri continued with disgust, "Too many Christians are pacifists, we need them to stop signing up for martyrdom, to stop hiding in forest and living like rats in the sewers and rise up to join the resistance. The time to fight is now. You must inspire them to join us Catherine, they will listen to you."

I abided, "I don't know that they will listen to me, but I will try."

"KhorOshaya moya dEvochka, do svidAniya Catherine." Yuri said proudly.

"Goodbye Yuri." I replied.

"I understood goodbye, but what did he say in Russian before that?" I asked

Peter smiled and he said, "He called you, 'good girl'."

"Hmm, and what does, 'dorogoy' mean?" I inquired.

Peter translated, "Dorogoy means, 'my dear' in Russian.

I sighed, "Well, I guess I better think about what message I will give. God help me." I got some paper and a pen and sat to write my speech.

Jacob smiled and assured me, "Seek the Spirit of Wisdom, she will guide you."

I recorded a video and I spoke each word slowly and clearly. I wanted to ensure it was well transmitted and clearly articulated. It felt painfully slow as I spoke, but it seemed wise to do so. I finished and I sent it to Eric.

I don't know how he made it go viral on the Internet, but he did. He also translated it into various languages via voice recognition and somehow it was my voice being streamed in Japanese, Mandarin, Russian, French, English, German, and others. Eric was a genius. Peter and I sat down and listened to it in English.

"Fellow comrades, my brothers and sisters, I am Commander Catherine Miles, one of many leaders in the resistance. Thanks to our commitment to humanity and freedom we have united, regardless of race, or religion, or nation, to stand against the self-proclaimed god Lumen and his puppet Augustus.

They have strived to rule the world through bribery, manipulation and terror.

We have succeeded in frustrating their plans to rule over the entire earth. They have been limited by our coordinated efforts across the globe, but we can no longer fight without your support. We need you.

We have managed, due to our extended networks and commitment thank God, to avoid the consequences of an all-out nuclear attack that was orchestrated by China.

You may fear the power of China and her agents of destruction, and you may be motivated out of fear to support the New World Order. You may be tempted to believe the lies that Lumen spared us all from nuclear annihilation. I assure you, he did not! Do not believe his lies; do not tremble before him!

Now is the time to rise up. Join us and stand against him!

For those brothers and sisters in China, India, Africa, North Korea and Russia, we know that it is your politicians that attempted to annihilate North America and the New World Order simultaneously. They did not succeed, and we the people will not tolerate a new dictator to arise. We will not submit to any form of dictatorship. We know the people of China are not responsible for the decisions of its political leaders and we can only hope that you rise up and hold them to account.

Our cells cover the earth, but we cannot defeat our enemies without your support. We need you to stop running, stop hiding, and stop complying. Resist these dictators with us. Join us and reclaim your freedom. The world is what we make it.

The choice is yours, but answer these questions, what kind of world do you want to live in? Do you want a dictatorship ruled by ruthless men, or a world of freedom, where we forge our own future, our own destiny?

The world is what we make it, but first we must take it back. Unite with us and help to win our freedom. If you embrace this ideal, then join us and know that you are not alone. Together we are strong. Join us and claim your freedom.

This is Catherine Miles commander of the Night Squad, signing off."

*****

I was filled with hope as John grew. Each day his joy allowed us to cultivate love. His birth brought us such rejuvenation. I felt like my spirit had been reborn again, like the child in me, long forgotten emerged once again.

John grew very fast. His aging appeared to be many times that of a normal child. He was the size of a large two year old at birth, and his intellectual development kept pace with his physical.

The winter in the mountains lasted so long, but it was nearly over and he was a small boy with an insatiable curiosity. By the time spring rains had fallen he looked like he could enter kindergarten.

I could not explain it, but I knew a change was coming with the season...

*****

Chapter Three: When Angels Come to Call

Twelve more months had passed since the nuclear attack. We continued our life in seclusion and serenity, until the day two men came to call. I did not know how they got there at first, but I assumed the president sent them. However, I could see that same aura of light which shone about Jacob and I as it shimmered about them as well. Later I discovered they came through a secret passageway, which led to the base of the mountain...

When they entered, they said, "Hello Jacob it is good to see you again."

Jacob replied, "Hello Nahor, hello Lazaro, this is Catherine, Peter, and of course this little man is John Raziel."

Nahor bent down and offered his hand to John and said, "Raziel I am pleased to meet you. You have a great name. Do you know what it means?"

John was brilliant, gifted and looked the size of six year old. He shook Nahor's hand and replied, "Yes I am a beloved gift from God and a secret of Jehovah."

Peter asked with surprise and suspicion, "John how did you know that?"

John simply replied, "You remember, Jacob told us when I was born."

We all looked on in amazement as John continued to converse with Nahor, "What does your name mean?"

Nahor smiled as he replied, "My name means, 'Breath of fire' and this is Lazaro." Nahor stood up and continued, "His name means, 'God is my help.' Our Creator named us well."

John asked, "Can you breathe fire Nahor?"

Nahor laughed, "Anything is possible with God, but my name is thus because the words from my mouth can burn to the heart and soul of man and melt his ice cold heart. It is a gift from the Creator."

Then John turned to Jacob and I and inquired, "Mommy, Jacob, what do your names mean?"

I smiled and picked up my son and answered, "I don't know; someone once told me he thought it meant something like, gift of God."

Jacob interjected, "It doesn't. It actually means, 'Pure'. That person was incorrect when he told that."

I laughed, "Pure, well I think I was misnamed then."

Peter grinned and my son hugged me and said, 'That's okay mommy, I love you and I'm your gift from God."

I kissed his head and said, "Yes you are, my son."

Jacob then told us, "My name means, 'follower' however, because of the biblical Jacob, people think it means, 'Holder of the heel'. I am a follower of the Most High."

I put John down and said, "Well enough with all this name business. You two may come in and sit and I will prepare supper. Any friends of Jacob are always welcome."

Peter followed me and said, "I'll help."
We both prepared them a feast.

I still recall them with a little awe. They were very tall and lean, but muscular, with perfectly chiseled features and they had a commanding presence. They had silken hair, which fell to their waist. The one named Nahor and he had golden hair, which shone like the sun, and stunning green eyes. The other, Lazaro, had hair as black as the night, and he had blue sapphire eyes, much like my own. I had never seen such beautiful men before and their perfection astounded me.

Over supper Peter inquired, "So tell us, who you are and why you're here."

Nahor answered, "We are angels of the Lord. The enemy will soon find you, and John must come with us for his own protection. We both will have charge over him. We will train him and shield him from the enemy until he is fully grown and equipped to fulfill his destiny."

Peter asked skeptically, "And what fortune is that and how did the enemy find us?"

John answered, "I am the secret of Jehovah Peter, a weapon in the war to come."

Peter smiled at John and said, "John, you are too young for this war child, no matter how fast you are growing."

Nahor spoke gently to Peter as he said, "Peter Joseph, John will not be fighting in this battle. The war scroll has been read from. Satan has broken the seal and attacked the lower levels of Heaven.

He failed, still, the Devil is determined to weaken our armies and reclaim the world of men. This is the battle John is being prepared to fight."

Peter sought clarification, "I thought you all believed Lumen and his puppet Augustus were attempting to do that now."

Lazaro tried to explain, "No Peter, the earth was just a diversion, a part of a greater plan. Satan wanted to wipe out the guardians who reside in the lower levels of the kingdom of Heaven. We rise up to report to God, but our responsibility is to guard men from demonic attacks and influences."

Peter looked skeptical, but he did not challenge their declarations. Lazaro placed a hand on my shoulder, "The war in the Heavens has been fierce, and it began when you were incarcerated. God has heard you Catherine, but the messengers where needed to report from the battle field."

"That's why heaven has been silent and I have not perceived the demonic." I understood as Lazaro nodded in response to my inference.

Nahor informed us, "We won that assault from Satan and his army, but our numbers have diminished. The demons now walk the Earth and so must our brethren. The Angels have not walked the Earth freely for centuries, but the time has come. Man cannot fight this battle alone."

Lazaro, "It is a terrifying prospect, but it is a necessary evil."

Peter challenged, "Why do you lament this, if it is true? Why do you call this evil?"

Jacob answered, "Because, we fear the return of the Nephilim."

Peter asked, "Who is that?"

I answered, "It is not who, but what; they are a race that is an offspring between angels and women."

Peter was shocked as he inquired, "You all sleep with humans?"

Nahor assured him, "No. It is forbidden, but in our human forms our heavenly fortitude diminishes and some of us succumbed to the flesh. This is why so many demonic rituals involve orgies. The demons are especially short on restraint and they do not value obedience to the law as we do."

Jacob added, "When an angelic being mates with a human, their children have supernatural abilities, powers that enable them to rise above mere mortals, or rule over them. It destroys the balance."

Peter inferred, "And along with it mankind's ability to live free from tyranny and oppression."

"Yes." Lazaro answered.

Peter looked at me and then asked Lazaro, "Is that what happened to Catherine? Is she a Nephilim?"

Jacob answered, "No Catherine's parents were mortal, but there are a few mortals who have an ancient lineage, a bloodline that can trace itself back to the Nephilim."

Lazaro informed us of the history, "We tried to wipe them out, but we did not kill any children who did not exhibit unique powers. We hunted them for a few generations and then centuries later the bloodline surfaced once again. The Nephilim decedent's powers were so diminished, their blood diluted, that they were no longer a threat to humanity. They were watched, but no longer hunted."

Peter asked, "Then why is Catherine so powerful, if she is just a decedent?"

Lazaro answered, "Her power is not from the bloodline alone. When a decedent of the Nephilim dies and crosses over to the other side, or even if they pierce the veil between life and death and return to earth their powers are enhanced, but Catherine was also given living water to drink by the Lord when she was in Heaven."

"So you're telling me her near death experience was real and I suppose this is what happened to Eric as well?" Peter scoffed.

Nahor answered, "Yes, Eric is a genius because of his lineage and since they killed him his powers and genius will continue to grow as well."

Jacob added, "Eric doesn't know, but we will soon have to inform him. A Nephilim is only as strong as the angel that sired them and their powers are evident in their gifting. Humans have seen them as the great warriors, geniuses, psychics and mages of history."

Lazaro smiled and placed a hand on Peter's shoulder as he added, "You wanted proof Peter, you are about to witness an era when angels and demons walk the Earth with men."

Peter declared, "I don't believe it."

Lazaro smiled, "You will."

Nahor called to John, "Raziel we must be going soon."

I was disturbed in my spirit and compelled to ask, "Lazaro, Nahor, who is the father of my lineage?"

They looked at each other and then to Jacob who answered, "Catherine, you are the adopted child of God and his chosen warrior, nothing else matters. You know that better than most. You're sealed and your name is written in the heavenly scroll."

Lazaro added, "Time is short we really must leave."

I did not want to let John go, but I knew we had to return to the war and John had to be safe and prepared to fulfill his purpose. Still, I held him close to me as he sat on my lap.

John wiped the tears from my face and he said, "It is going to be okay Mommy, please don't cry. I will see you again. I'll just be gone for a little while. It will be fun, like a great adventure."

I kissed his forehead and he continued to speak asking, "Nahor, Lazaro will you teach me to fight like Mommy, Peter and Jacob."

Lazaro replied, "Better, John you will become the greatest warrior mankind has ever known."

"Really" John replied with excitement.

"Really" confirmed Nahor.

"Wow, will I get to fight with swords, bows and arrows?" John asked excitedly.

Nahor answered, "Yes and many other weapons too, but you will eventually be gifted with one weapon designed just for you."

"I can't wait, did you hear that Mommy, my own special weapon. When do we leave?" John inquired.

"We could leave right now." Nahor answered.

John smiled and then he frowned and asked, "Okay, but can we have dessert first?"

Lazaro looked pleased and said, "Yes, I think we should have dessert."

They ate and then Nahor warned us, "You should prepare to leave as well, for the enemy has discovered your location and is closing in on you."

I nodded and I replied, "Thank you, we will prepare to depart immediately."

Nahor placed his hand on Peter's shoulder and said, "Don't be frustrated in the difficult journey you have in finding God, the treasure you will find is greater than any other known to man, but know this, until you are prepared to stand naked before God and man and not be ashamed, you cannot enter into the kingdom of our Lord."

"I do hope you're not speaking literally, Nahor." Peter retorted

Nahor laughed, "No, not literally little brother, but the spirit of truth is inside you, you must look at your heart and soul and see yourself as you really are and then will be able to see clearly.

Know yourself Peter and then you will know you too are a child of God. You are about to witness things that could drive some men mad, but when you wrestle with the child within and win, look toward your real father who is creator of all and you will not be afraid. Prepare yourself Peter; you never know when an angel will come to call."

Peter did not know how to respond, so he said nothing, but he nodded and shook Nahor's hand. After that I hugged and kissed my son goodbye. I feared that I would not see them again for many years. I knew that we would probably not see John again, until he was a young man.

As they turned to leavé Peter asked, "Hey, you two, you never answered, how did the enemy find out where we were?"

Lazaro answered, "You have a traitor in the rebellion."

Peter frowned as he pondered, "Our own personal Judas, huh; how ironic is that?"

Nahor responded, "Not ironic, it is simply history repeating itself."

"History will not repeat itself Nahor. We will make our own destiny." Peter said resolutely.

Lazaro grinned as Peter placed his arm around me. Nahor remained serious as he warned, "Be on guard Peter, God bless all of you." Then Lazaro kissed my forehead and added, "Go with God."

I was comforted by his touch and from knowing that my son was in the hands God and under of the protection of the angels. Still, a deep emptiness and lament remained within my soul knowing that our solitude and seclusion came to an end.

******

Chapter Four: In the Dark of the Night

I remembered that on the night that John left, as we were packing, Peter got a message from Eric, he informed us that Augustus suspected where we were and he would likely be sending troops by morning.

Peter thanked Eric for the information and then told Eric, "Eric, I want you to do three things for me."

"Anything Captain, what is it?" Eric replied.

"Check the status on an old project called, Star Wars, renamed, Project Cosmos." Peter demanded.

"Roger that. Anything else, Captain?" Eric questioned.

"Yes, I would also like all information pertaining to the perimeter defense system, especially concerning the shield technology under the code name, Scutum Contego. Finally I need you to go over the past few months of internet communiques coming in and out of the camps and among our leadership. I need you to find anything suspicious. We have a breech in security."

"Do we have a traitor Captain?" Eric asked plainly.

"Yes, and they have to be very high in the chain of command, so be careful and this is for my eyes only." Peter said sternly.

"Don't worry Captain, I'm on it." Eric assured him.

"Thanks Eric, Signing off." Peter looked deeply troubled.

I said, "Don't worry Peter, all will be well. Who do you fear it is?"

Peter looked down at me and hugged me as he replied, "Only a few people know where we are. Jacob, Nahor, Lazaro, Eric, you and I, young John and..."

Peter couldn't finish and I protested, "I assure you, it's not Sayid."

Peter said gently, "There is no point speculating about it now, but he is the only other person who knew our location, or our location wasn't as secure as we thought. Regardless, it's time to move out. Let's go."

Peter kissed my forehead and we prepared to depart.

*****

We grabbed our survival gear and made our way down the secret passage of the mountain. As we made our way down the corridor I was contemplating how I would miss the daily mountain climbs.

We had climbing gear and every day, despite the weather conditions we would propel down the face of the mountain by our balcony and rock climb up again. We should have left that way, but it was still too dark when we left.

As we walk down the secret passage, I was glad that we were prepared to fight if we had to. You couldn't even tell that I had a child.

I lost myself in a memory as we descended the mountain. I smiled as I remembered what occurred only a few days earlier. We were working out in the gym and I couldn't help, but take pleasure in Peter's admiration of me as I did one arm pull-ups.

That night, after showering he said, "Catherine you are amazing." He didn't have his shirt on and I couldn't help but stare.

I had just a towel about me as I returned from my shower as he took me in his arms and inquired, "Catherine when are you going to marry me?"

I knew that we were probably now in the End Times. The Tribulation was drawing to a close and the Lord's wrath had been falling upon the earth as the war in the heavens was being waged and yet, I was not concerned with that at all.

I desired Peter; he was so gorgeous, so irresistible. I wanted him so badly; I longed to be his wife. He would be mine, my husband. I knew he had already waited a long time for me.

I did not know how much longer I could hold myself back. My mind took pleasure at the thought of having him, taking him and then I laughed out loud, ending the memory.

Peter asked, "What's so funny?"

"Oh nothing, I was just laughing at the meaning of my name, 'Purity.' I was definitely misnamed." I replied,

It was very dark in the passageway and I was in front of him, so I could not see his reaction, but I heard him chuckle slightly and he said, "As long as those impure thoughts you are having are about me and not about those two pretty boys."

I stopped and turned towards him with my flashlight and replied, "You're not jealous are you?"

He took me in his arms and said, "That depends, are you thinking about me?"

I kissed him long and slow and then I assured him, "Yes, I was thinking about you."

He smiled and said, "Good, you can tell me later what you were thinking."

Then Jacob let out a sigh and said, "You two really do need to get married."

"I know big guy, that's what I keep telling her." Peter quickly agreed.

I turned and said, "Enough you two. I agree. A new chapter in our lives is about to begin. I want us to begin it as husband and wife, but we have to do it right, legally and with witnesses."

I was surprised by my own reply, but I stated honestly, "I don't know for sure, but I sense that we will have the opportunity to marry soon. I can't explain it. It is just a feeling I have, we will find the right person to marry us. Don't worry Peter my love, the time will come."

Peter looked a little suspicious so I added, "I will marry you as soon as we find someone to marry us and we have witnesses. Agreed?"

"Agreed" He was content knowing I would be his wife. If only the war would end.

Jacob chastised Peter gently saying, "By the way Peter, those boys as you called them are much older than you. I knew them before the world began."

I don't think Peter believed him, but he made no response as we continued to descend the mountain through dark places. I was sure this journey would evoke painful memories that should have been forgotten. I faced my fear of dark places, thankful for our flashlights and strengthened by the Spirit within me.

I led the way down the dark twisting path before us. It was a difficult and perilous journey through the long narrow passageway. The depth of darkness around us was greater than any I have witnessed thus far. It was darker than a moonless night where at least we were comforted by the stars to guide us.

The little light we initially had was only provided by the narrow doorway behind us and our flashlights, but as we continued that light from the doorway faded. Then our flashlights slowly dimmed as well.

Jacob and I had the ability to see, our eyes adjusted well in the darkness, but I feared for Peter. He would not be able to see at all.

I stopped and grabbed Peter's arm as he made his protests known with but a whisper, which is too easily heard when enclosed by silence. "Catherine we can't continue this way. It's too dark to see and the path is perilous. This is foolishness. We must go back. We can use our climbing gear and climb down the mountain side when the sun rises."

I replied gently, "I don't think there's time for that. I will lead you Peter and Jacob will follow. I have the everlasting light within me, to which the darkness must give way."

"I am not talking of spiritual things Catherine, but of the physical. We cannot know the way if we can't see it." He said this with a harsh whisper, which rang out far louder than he had intended.

I turned around and he looked at me. He stumbled backward in fear as he probably noticed my eyes were shining brightly much like a cat's eyes. As he fumbled his way rearward, he backed into Jacob. He turned and noted his eyes shone brilliantly as well.

Peter asked, "Are you both genetically altered? Tell me the truth."

I reminded him, "We have already answered that question before Peter, we were not genetically altered we are made this way by God."

Peter rationalized, "Well, I guess I can accept that after seeing you two and John that evolution has taken a giant leap forward, or backward, I suppose being a genetic throwback is more likely, it would certainly explain why Jacob is like the giants in myths and legends. Jacob are you one of these Nephilim decedents too?"

Jacob answered, "No Peter, I am not a half breed. No offence Catherine."

Catherine, "Too late Jacob, offence taken, but I forgive you."

Peter queried, "Then why do your eyes glow in the dark? What are you Jacob?"

Jacob answered, "I am Catherine's guardian angel."

Peter scoffed, "If you and your buddies truly are angels then where are your wings?"

Jacob laughed, "Peter you are incorrigible; all angels don't have wings and I am in my human form. If you think I am large now, well my true size would astound you."

Peter didn't argue and I interjected, "Okay Peter, do you have any night vision goggles at the bottom of your pack?"

"No, I left them with the resistance fighters. They were running short on supplies." He replied.

I ordered, "Stay close, put your hand on my shoulder and walk slowly. I can see."

It would be a difficult decent. He found it unnerving walk through the darkness for him and then my visions of Hell came to mind. I was haunted as the pictures of that nightmare flashed before my mind's eye. I refused to allow fear to consume me.

Peter once told me that he used to call the darkness his friend, when he led attacks against the enemy. It was in the darkness where he sought its solitude, but now that the darkness was so thick all around us, how would he feel?

The pace of my breathing quickened and I soon feared I wouldn't be able to breathe at all.

Peter asked, "Catherine, are you alright?"

"Yes, I can see, it is just stupid memories rising to the surface. I'm alright." I assured him as I took a deep breath.

Then I was paralyzed with fear, as I felt some hellish spirit brush past me. Though I could see nothing I knew it was there. I felt as if it were circling me. I sensed it as an ice-cold breeze. I could no longer find my voice. If I could have, I would surely have screamed. I was letting my vision of Hell fill my mind and I feared I was hallucinating. I was being driven mad by the memories of the darkness.

I took another deep breath and I heard the Lord say to me in my mind, "Be not afraid, for I am with you. I am the Light that shines in the darkness, so do not fear child."

I then said, "Don't worry love, I'm okay." Then in an ancient tongue I uttered these words, "Boreh d'bwaschmâja Nethkâdasch schmach row"

Jacob translated, "She prays, 'Creator, who fills all realms of sound, light and vibration, may your light be experienced, my utmost holiest, shine.' She prays forth the word again."

Then my radiance grew as a soft light began to emanate from my being, much like the light I saw surrounding the angels. I didn't always see this glow about Jacob and me, but at times I did and after praying these words he shone brightly as well.

I remember Peter once believed that in darkness there is no shadow, for there is no light. Now, as I walked before him in the darkness descending the mountain and the light which shone about me would have cast Peter's shadow upon the walls, but Jacob shone behind Peter and I smiled, realizing that he was walking in the light. The darkness gave way and now that we shone so, no shadows remained.

The light that emanated from our bodies provided enough light to allow Peter to see the path before our feet and he became surefooted. The path was steep before us and as we descended down the mountain I sensed a darker world all around me, but I felt safe with Jacob as my rear guard.

I would often pray for Peter to find faith in Christ and I knew I was given faith by God. He enabled me to stand firm even when the whole world appeared to be falling apart.

I always believed there was hope in the darkness and a source of light to be found amidst the shadows of our lives, but I also understood that Peter was right too. Life was what we make it.

The future for me was chosen, a result of choice and consequence, action and reaction, as well as a woven tapestry. It was a predestined life too, part of a divine design, at least for the chosen ones. Peter was a part of that plan. We each had a role to play, I was grateful that we could share in it together.

My thoughts expressed trepidation about the war, the coming battle and this hell on earth. With men like Augustus and Satan's delusional religious followers still in power, I could easily understand why Peter could not believe that God was in control.

I hated that a man like Augustus could rise to power. I did not understand why this was part of a divine plan, a destiny written long ago. No, I could not understand it either, how could I ever expect Peter to.

He once asked me, "What kind of God would allow such a thing to occur, let alone plan such a thing?"

I answered, "God did not plan for Satan to rise to power, any more than men like Hitler and Augustus. No, he simply foresaw it, he warned us and he made a plan using people like you and me to fight against it."

Peter would not believe it, and I would not argue with him about it either. Such arguments were futile. I didn't have any adequate answers for him and yet I understood his logic and his struggle with faith.

I would just have to leave him in God's hands and remind myself, 'It is God's job to save him and my pleasure to love him.' I really did love him and I couldn't wait to marry him.

We reached the base of the mountain. As the ground became level. I could feel a fresh gentle breeze upon my skin as fresh air filled my lungs. I breathed deeply.

We could see a narrow slit of light just ahead and heard a rushing of water nearby. We made our way through the narrow passageway for some time enabling our eyes to slowly become accustomed to the light without any discomfort to our sight. Then the passageway opened into a broad opening beneath a waterfall.

The mist in the air refreshed our skin and the early morning sunlight shone through, dancing upon the droplets in the air. We all took a moment to take in the fleeting pleasure of the beauty, which lay before us. I had some deep sense of foreboding that I could not shake, but I knew we had to return to war.

Peter's parents were soldiers and he had been a Marine since youth. Fighting was in his blood. From the time he was a child, it was second nature to him, and like me he spent far more time away from home at private military schools and summer camps then with his parents. It was sad, he hardly knew them.

We were both closer to our friends then we were ever to our families of origin. We were especially disconnected from our earthly fathers; both of whom were harsh and closed off men, who never really let us in. Our fathers never treasured us; they never celebrated our gifts, talents, or accomplishments.

Peter once told me, "No matter how far I excelled, although my dad publicly proclaimed he was proud of me, he never spent time getting to know me. When he was with me, all he did was lecture and criticize me. It was impossible to please him and I accepted long ago that I could never live up to his expectations. I also realized that even though I was his son by blood, I would never know him as a father. As I grew older, I no longer even cared that I wouldn't and I became my own man without him."

I understood that somehow in this, Peter probably had a hard time seeing God as his Father, because of his experience with his earthly dad. How could he accept God's proclamations of love for us when he appeared to be so distant? How could Peter accept that his true father cares and is involved in his life when his earthly father was not?

Peter was about to truly witness a world filled with angels and I feared demons, surely that would entice him to seek God. Wouldn't it? No, God would have to prove himself to Peter.

We both knew little family intimacy and little peace growing up, but these past few months in the wilderness were filled with happiness and a serenity we had never known before. This peace that was once so foreign to both of us, now united us together as we gazed at the beauty of the waterfall before us. I was pained to think it was to war we must return.

Jacob placed his large arm about Peter's shoulders and said, "This is just a taste of the beauty of heaven."

Then I added, "Remember this peace and magnificent beauty Peter, for now we must face a deeper darkness and battle something far more disturbing than anything you have battled before."

The three of us emerged from beneath the waterfall and made our way from the majestic mountains and journeyed toward the bloodshed, toward the battle, where armies from two worlds would collide.

As we made our way through the valleys, along the banks of the crystal stream, we ran most of the day and we felt a menacing presence on all sides of us. We were being followed by shadows, which clung to the protection provided by the forest.

A large flock of crows circled above us, but they fled as they heard an eagle's cry from high above them to the east of us, riding the rising warmth of the air. Jacob warned, "The animals following us are the Devil's spies."

Jacob spoke to us as we prepared to bed down for the night. He said motioning to the eyes glowing in the darkness, "When the demons took corporeal form, as Sayid witnessed, they began to roam the earth in large numbers as man, but now as the final battle draws near they are in many wild beasts as well. So sleep and I will stand guard for your mortal bodies require rest tonight."

We awoke despite Jacob's vigilance to the horrid shrill yipping of coyotes closing in on us. I was surprised when I woke to find a silver bow and quiver filled with arrows beside me.

I looked around and I noted Jacob had a shining sword too. It was almost as long as I, but it was perfect for his stature. Peter had two weapons near him, a dagger and a saber. I did not know not from where they came, but Jacob informed us, "We were each given a weapon from heaven's store room. The Lord felt Peter needed two." Jacob shrugged his shoulders and then turned his attention toward the forest.

I could see dozens of eyes that glowed from the shadows of the forest. I drew my bow and took aim as we began to battle the demons within these wicked creatures of the night.

They emerged from the shadows and though we easily slay many of the beasts they did not retreat, nor shrink back in fear.

Peter raised an eyebrow as he eyed the sword and dagger. He did not grab either; rather he shot many with his pistols that were always at his side. He smiled, "I prefer modern weapons to archaic ones."

He killed many; nevertheless they kept coming at us, as an onslaught of demonic coyotes attacked.

I spoke out a command in the ancient tongue. I said, "In the name of the Lord I call upon noble creatures of the night to come and wage war on the enemies of your God."

The timber wolves howled a reply as the demonic coyotes closed in. As we became bathed in the demons' blood a large pack of wolves attacked the vile creatures. Soon we stood victorious and I witnessed a great earthquake. The wolves backed up as those we had slain along with the few remaining coyotes were snarling and gnashing one another as they were sucked into the earth.

We made our way to the edge of the river and we washed the blood from our hands and faces, then Jacob declared, "Hurry we must quicken our pace, we must reach Jerusalem before the next full moon."

We packed up quickly, but before we left I turned to smile at the Alpha male of the wolf pack. It was the same white wolf I met before the winter. I knelt on one knee to the ground and the wolf came before me. I stoked his chest, and I thanked him. Then I got up to run. The wolf pack ran into the forest and followed us for three days, as our guardians.

*****

The next day we came to a town named Troy nestled in the mountains. We walked along the edge of the road steering ourselves away from the town. One day we were walking the edge of the forest when we saw a military convoy on a divided highway below us.

We hid ourselves quickly amidst some pines and when we took out our binoculars Peter said, "I don't believe it."

Peter handed me the binoculars and I looked and said, "It's Sayid."

Sayid was sitting in the front seat of one of the trucks at the head of the convoy.

We ran along the road above them until we came to a bridge and then we jumped upon the last vehicle that was carrying supplies. Two soldiers were riding in the back and would have shot us had not both Jacob and I moved quickly to disarm them.

Peter held his weapon to the driver's head and ordered, "Radio ahead tell them we need to stop, but keep the motor's running."

The soldier did not comply, and then I later heard that Peter said, "Why does everything have to be so hard?" He punched the driver so hard that he was dazed and the soldier in the passenger seat grabbed the wheel and steered it straight and thankfully the driver's foot was no longer on the gas. The soldier in the passenger seat got the truck under control and then the driver regained his senses.

Peter said, "Now are you going to comply, or do I need to be more persuasive?"

The young soldier replied, "That won't be necessary, but you have no idea what you're up against."

Peter responded, "Kid, I know exactly what I'm up against. Now radio ahead and come to a gentle stop."

The convoy came to a sudden stop and soldiers filed out from the back of the trucks, aiming their weapons at Peter. He had to raise his hands and surrender.

Meanwhile Jacob and I were in the back of the vehicle, we had disarmed the young soldiers with ease. I looked carefully at the weapon in my hands. I smiled as I recognized Eric's handiwork.

I tossed the gun back to the young soldier, which he immediately aimed at me. Jacob did not surrender his weapon, but he warned the boy, "I wouldn't do that if I were you."

For some inexplicable reason I trusted that the boy would not fire. The young soldier assumed we were the enemy and Jacob warned, "He's going to shoot."

Before the boy could pull the trigger I kicked the gun up with lighting fast speed again; I grabbed the riffle from the air and aimed it at the boy and said, "Listen, I don't want to hurt you so behave and don't try anything stupid. We're on your side."

The boy then recognized me, "Commander Miles, is that you?"

I nodded and the soldier continued, "I am so sorry. Shit, I could've killed you! Forgive me, mam."

Jacob chuckled, "You could have tried, but it would have been to your own peril."

I looked at Jacob and grinned and then I handed the soldier his weapon and said, "You are a very brave young man."

"Thank you, Commander." He beamed as he took back his weapon.

The convoy came to a halt and soldiers pointing their weapons at us immediately surrounded the truck. They were far too eager to fire and I thought they would, when finally Sayid appeared.

He saw Peter first with his hands in the air and Sayid ordered, "Lower your weapons!" They all obeyed him without hesitation.

We jumped down and embraced him one at a time. Patting each other's back everyone made their way back to their truck as Sayid led us to one filled with soldiers and came in to sit with us.

I noticed the wolves were standing ready at the edge of the forest and Jacob held up his hand. I grinned again as the wolves disappeared into the forest.

Sayid briefed us on all that had developed since we last saw him. He said, "Oh it is so good to see you again. You will bring much confidence to the forces when they find out it is you Commander. You can lead us in the final battle."

I smiled and touched his hand and asked, "How is Eric? Have you seen him?"

Sayid beamed, "Oh, yes, yes, he is known throughout North America as a hero. If it were not for him, America would have been destroyed in that nuclear attack. I don't know what technology he employed to change the winds, or how he stopped the tidal waves, but the perimeter defense system worked like a charm."

Jacob interjected, "It was…" I placed my hand on Jacob and silenced him with a look.

Then I said, "Please, continue Sayid."
He did continue, but he looked curious, as if he wanted to know what Jacob was about to say. Instead it was Sayid who spoke; "Well, we all know that very few people in North America actually received the microchip and resistance grew like a roaring thunder after we were attacked by nuclear forces.

We in the resistance feared that the backlash from knowing it was those countries that opposed Augustus whom attacked us would cause more Americans to support him. However, praise be to Allah they did not.

The president also convinced most of North America and South America to unite and take our freedom back.

After your speech on the Internet, people from everywhere joined our underground cells, so many in fact that we came out of hiding. America is largely under American control again; however we are constantly on guard from betrayal from within and President Davidson is still attempting diplomatic negotiations with Augustus.

"That is quite evident." Peter interrupted.

"What do you mean?" Sayid inquired

"I'll tell you later, please continue." I replied as Sayid studied our facial expressions for a moment. Peter looked angry and disturbed.

Sayid continued, "The people across the globe from every nation have claimed they have had visions and dreams of angels appearing to them, encouraging them to unite and fight the enemy Augustus and his false god. They say God poured out his Spirit and sent countless legions of angels to inform those who did not know that the end of the war was near, but we have to unite to defeat the enemy"

I was somewhat astonished at the words that proceeded from Peter's lips, "Then I saw another angel flying in the midst of heaven, having the everlasting gospel to preach to those who dwell on the earth, to every nation, tribe, tongue and people. Revelation 14:6."

I kissed his lips and Jacob patted his back. He looked dismayed for he didn't speak of his own accord. He did not tell Sayid he was still not a believer and I could tell that it bothered him that he didn't know where that came from. He knew it was scripture, but he did not know why he had uttered it.

Sayid laughed and clapped his hands and declared, "Praise be to Allah, the Living God and Most High my brother."

Peter frowned and Sayid continued to give us his update. "We have spent the past several months killing the evil dictator's forces. Now that America has been secured we are joining the armies for the final battle against Augustus. We will be shipping out in three days."

Catherine spoke a firm warning to us, "Sayid we will be fighting the forces of extraordinary strength and skill. Some of the men in Augustus' forces are no longer humans, they are demons. They are fighting for their very existence and they will not fall easily. We will also face millions of genetically enhanced soldiers. They are better than the first models."

"Eric informed me Catherine, he has recruited many of them, they want freedom too, and they resent the devil that created them to be slaves. Eric has befriended Servant 678 and Augustus has no idea how many in his ranks are willing to betray him.

You were also correct about the dictator's unwillingness to focus any energy on saving the lives of his first group of genetically enhanced soldiers. He simply used them until the cancer weakened them and killed them.

Sky has found a cure, he injects a lethal virus that makes the soldier sick for six weeks as his body battles a flu like infection and the virus targets the cancer cells, leaving the patients normal cellular structures unharmed, then he uses a combined injection designed from both servant 678's DNA and yours to boost their antibodies and kill the virus.

He has found something in your DNA to slow the aging process in soldiers like 678. He is finding it difficult to isolate, but he is still working on it. Still, the tide has turned Catherine. We are about to engage in our final victory."

Peter was pleased, but not fully convinced and then Jacob added, "Furthermore what few will actually see are legions of angels that will also be engaged in the final battle. Keep the faith Sayid for God is with us, but we must be strong for millions of us will die in combat. Be not afraid; for we will engage in the greatest conflict that mankind has ever seen, the battle where two worlds will collide. "

Sayid smiled and said, "Yes, I believe this war will cost many lives, but so many of Augustus's first soldiers are joining us that all is well. I thank Eric for that. They are infiltrating more of the newer models even as we speak.

We meet up with Eric tomorrow; I will let him report to you. It is awesome news and amazing developments, but I will say no more. He should have had the honor of telling you."

I never saw Sayid so animated and excited. In this darkness he was filled with optimism. He focused on the light that shone in this miserable world. I did not want to blacken his mood, but we had to question him about the traitor among us.

"Sayid, we need to talk about a betrayal, perhaps a spy in our midst." I said seriously.

"Someone leaked our location to Augustus or Lumen." His forces came to attack us, what do you know of this?" Peter asked directly, staring intently at Sayid.

Sayid looked confused and then troubled and then angry as he uttered, "Bay-waqoof, bay-waqoof, haasid oarat."

Peter replied, "Mary, why would she betray us?"

Sayid sighed and ran his fingers thorough his hair as he explained, "I am sorry Commander, and I never thought she would ever betray us. She has always been jealous of you Catherine, and she hated my devotion to you. Stupid woman! I thought her realization of your love for the Captain would have quieted her foolish suspicions. I will handle this and I am very ashamed and sorry. I promise you that I will never divulge any information to her again. Ghudal madad karnaa mujhayhad ."

Sayid did not use his mother tongue often, but I had heard him utter it, whenever he was extremely frustrated or angry. I did not understand him, but Peter told me later what he said. Basically Sayid called Mary a stupid, foolish and jealous woman and then later said, "God help me." Sayid spoke in Arabic at times, but this was his Father's language, Urdu.

I was confident Sayid would handle the leak and we knew that he was angry with Mary, but I gave it no further thought. I knew that he was innocent and would never betray me.

I had one witness and tomorrow I would have my second. I would marry Peter before we had to face battle. This is where my thoughts resided, little else consumed me.

*****

We drove all through the night and Jacob was driving now. Peter and I were in the front seat and I was resting in Peter's arms. My heart burned from within, it was as if my soul leaped for joy as I saw a figure ahead of us walking along the road.

The headlights illuminated him with a blue hue. He looked like an angel, but he was far too small in stature and I knew that he was just a man.

I touched Jacob's arm and we came to a stop. The figure turned around he had long brownish blond wavy hair that fell like a main about his shoulders, he had a long beard and mustache too, but in my heart I knew him even if my eyes did not recognize him at first.

We got out of the trucks Sayid had his weapon raised and I ordered, "Lower your gun Sayid."

Jacob was at one side of me and Peter was on the other, and he had drawn his weapon as well, but would not lower it. We approached the man slowly. He had his hands guarding his eyes from the headlights.

As we came closer he said, "Catherine, is that you?"

I recognized his voice in an instant even though it was a little raw.

I uttered cautiously, "John it's me. Is it really you? I can't believe my eyes."

Peter whispered, "Catherine, don't be crazy he is too old to be your son, look at him."

"Not John my son, it's Brother John from Ireland, he returned to Canada and from the looks of things he has been in the Rockies for many years." I went up to him and he held me so tight, it was as if he would never let me go.

Peter put his gun away and said, "Hello Brother John; do you remember me?"

John looked at him and then to me and said, "Captain...Captain..."

Peter offered him his hand and said, "Roberts, but you can call me Peter."

John took his hand and smiled, "Hello Peter, yes I do remember you, from Ireland, the night you saved Catherine before departing for battle."

"Yes that's me." Peter answered

Sayid interrupted and said, "Sorry, please forgive me, but we must continue our journey. Can we move this reunion to the back of the truck?"

"Of course, come with me John." I ordered as I took one arm and looked to Peter and without a word asked him to take the other. John was skinny and weak, probably from years of fasting. We helped him up into the back of the truck.

"You look very hungry, would you like some food." I inquired and he nodded, yes. Sayid passed him a protein bar and enriched water.

After he finished Peter asked, "How long have you been in the mountains?"

John replied, "Ever since Catherine left Ireland and I heard her plane crashed in the ocean. It was all over the news. I went immediately to Canada and I made my way by foot deep into the heart of the Rockies and I never looked back, until today."

Peter said, "So..." Peter cleared his throat and asked, "Did you attend a funeral for her first, before you went into the mountains?"

"No" John replied honestly and then he inquired, "Why do you ask?"

Peter glanced at me a little unsure and answered John saying, "Well, I ask because Catherine had what you could label a, 'near death experience' when the plane went down and she says she saw you at her funeral."

John mused and replied, "I was not at her funeral, but I dreamed about her for many weeks after the plane crashed. She was in flames and torment, and at other times she was wet and cold.

I prayed for her often fearing she was in purgatory and then one day my dreams turned to joy. She was alive again laughing and playing and singing. I knew she was okay after that, but I assumed she had died and went on to heaven."

I looked at Peter as I said, "I did go to Heaven John, and Peter does not believe my experience was real. He believes it was all a cruel fabrication of a mind in trauma, or a comma induced dream. Regardless, thank you for your prayers, but I never saw purgatory. I was in Hell prior to seeing Heaven."

I touched John's hand and he smiled at me and declared, "Thank God you're alive Catherine; I'm so happy to see you. I was elated to see the light shining at me in the dark of night. I was so hungry and tired. I didn't know if I could walk another step."

"Then you eat and go to sleep John, we will talk when you wake." I assured him.

John replied, "I am usually up all night and I sleep by day, so I will just have a quick nap. I am more physically exhausted then mentally."

"Well rest, brother John, we will be here when you arise." Peter assured him as he placed his arm around me and I nestled into the crook of his arm.

Peter whispered in my ear as John drifted off to sleep, "So, have we found the man to marry us?"

I looked up at him, I kissed him and then I replied, "I believe so my love."

Peter smiled and I settled in his embrace and we both drifted off to sleep and drove on in the dark of the night.

*****

Chapter Five: A Deeper Understanding

I woke up to hear Peter and John conversing. John had just said, "So you're a Deist then?"

Peter answered him, "Yes, you could call me that. I have witnessed some amazing things that I have a limited rational explanation for. I believe that due to the immense complexity and intricacies of the known universe that a creative entity exists. I just don't embrace mankind's religious, and I would argue limited and warped view of him. I don't believe God is interactive. The world is what we make it."

John agreed, "You are correct, many of us do have a limited and warped view of God and he is the Creator of all that is seen and unseen. Humanity is prone to a very flawed and skewed perspective of God."

"So I take it that you, being a Catholic, believe as Catherine does?" Peter questioned.

John replied, "I do not know exactly what Catherine believes, since I knew her long ago. I presume her view of God has evolved, as has mine."

Peter said, "I thought God being perfect was unchanging"

John smiled as he said, "Yes he is, but our understanding and knowledge of him is not. He said,

'Seek and you will find' Peter. My years of searching for him and truth in the wilderness have deepened my understanding of him tremendously. I am transformed by it. God is so big and so deep; he is love, he is truth and we only get to know a small part of him.

Take Jesus for instance. The bible says that God is love and truth. Jesus said things like, 'I am the way, the truth and the light, anyone who believes in me will not expire, but will have perpetual life.' He also called himself the, 'bread of life' and 'wine,' and that we should feed on him, the bread that came from Heaven. He is the word of God that dwells within us. He also refers to himself as the vine and we are branches. Now some Christians try to take his words literally and some take them figuratively.

He loved to speak through symbols layered with meaning, but they can all be summed up in this way, when we follow his example daily, feeding the hungry, helping our fellow man without asking anything in return, then we are walking in love. We are love, one with God. When we love and accept each other, we are in the anointing and he is in us. When we live in the truth, speak truth, and when we can be open and honest with each other and do not judge each other, we are one with love. This is the heart of God.

Believe in love. Believe in truth, practice non judgment and love every day throughout your life and you will truly live. By turning from our wrong way of being and following him, otherwise known as repentance, accepting him, we live not only in this world, but the next as well."

Peter pondered this for a moment and inquired, "So, could the bible have meant that one day every knee will bow, one day every tongue will confess that truth, love, life is Lord? What is the actual meaning of the word Lord from the Greek?"

John replied, "This I believe this is literal as well as figurative. Lord refers to a judge, or a person with authority. The scripture reads, 'As surely as I live, says the Lord (the judge), every knee will bow before me; every tongue will confess to God;' so then each one of us will give an account of himself to God. Therefore let us stop passing judgment on one another...' It is from the book of Romans.

Peter said, "I can hope toward a day when truth, non-judgment and love reigns, I can even believe we will give account for our lives before a Creator who judges us, and that we must be honest and open before him, but the actual personage of Jesus as that judge and the king who returns, I don't know. I would have to see it to believe it."

John smiled and mused, "It's a start, to find God you must first believe he exists and then trust that he is good. As a Deist you are on your way. I believe more often than not we do not find God, rather he reveals himself to us. He will show himself to you when the time is right."

I stretched and yawned, "John gives you a lot to think about. I missed hearing your perspective John."

"Good morning Catherine" John smiled as he sat cross legged in the middle of the truck before me.

I laughed and noted, "John, you look like new age guru. We have to get rid of that hair on your face. I like the hair on your head though."

Peter teased me, "I knew it. You have a thing for long hair don't you?"

I smiled and said, "I like to run my fingers through it." I ran mine through his and kissed his lips.

Peter grinned and then had a slight furrow of his brow as he chided, "Hmm, maybe I should have been jealous of those two men with their long silken hair after all."

"Nonsense, I only have eyes for you." I assured him

John remarked, "You are a lucky man Peter, are you two married?"

"Not yet, but we were hoping you could rectify that." Peter said with a glimmer in his eye.

John smiled and said apologetically, "I can't, I never took my final vows."

Peter looked only slightly dismayed and then he said, "That's okay you can stand as our second witness, Sayid I assume you will be the other."

Sayid was very pleased and replied, "Of course I will, it will be an honor."

"Excellent, now all we need is to find your preacher Catherine." Peter looked to me and stated, "There is likely to be a Chaplin on the ship, will he do?

I smiled, "Yes, Peter he will do." Peter kissed me and the men on our truck cheered as we rolled to a stop. We had to refuel.

I took the opportunity to go in and borrow a pair of scissors, and a razor for John from one of Sayid's men. I gave them to him and remarked, "You really have to go clean yourself up. Here John, let me know if you need anything else."

"You certainly haven't changed all that much since I saw you last." John said scornfully.

"Under all that fur, I'd guess you haven't either." I retorted.

John laughed and made his way to the bathroom. I went to the women's and cleaned up as well. The other soldiers all washed up quickly in the river nearby, but they had to wait for us. John and I took much longer. They were all waiting patiently in the truck as we returned.

We both returned to the truck and looked, refreshed and clean. John had clean shaven face, we used soap foam to wash up and clean our hair and the hand dryers dried it. I lent him my brush when I was done. He looked magnificent, like the John I remembered.

Sayid commented, "Alright you two look beautiful, are you ready to go now?"

I patted his shoulder and said, "Isn't there a saying that cleanliness is next to godliness?"

Sayid smirked, "Very funny, Catherine."

Peter helped me up and as he took my hand he said, "She does look rather angelic. You're beautiful, Catherine."

I smiled and kissed his cheek. I never got tired of hearing his praises; I cared nothing for anyone else's, but his comments made me want to kiss him passionately. I didn't, I restrained myself, but I didn't stop myself from thinking about it.

Peter put his arm around me and the trucks started up once again. I caught Sayid frowning and looking at my stomach.

Sayid shared, "Mary is with child."

"Congratulations." I said with all sincerity.

Sayid looked down unsure how to ask and then decided not to, so I offered the information, "You are wondering about my son?"

Peter shook his head slightly, but I trusted Sayid, "He is a healthy boy, he is strong and smart and he is growing at a fantastic speed. When he left us he was the physical size of a five year old and very intelligent. He will never be found by the enemy. He is living in safety and seclusion with trusted caregivers."

Sayid looked relieved and then he commented, "I am glad to hear it. What did you name him?"

Peter answered, "John, I believe she named him after you." Peter said this as he stared at John across from us.

"Really, you two had a son and you named him after me." John beamed.

Peter answered coldly void of emotion as he replied factually, "He was not my son. It is a long story that I am sure Catherine will share with you, but let me summarize it by saying; the government had genetically enhanced soldiers rape her, they impregnated her in the hopes of creating a super soldier and using him as a pawn, as a weapon in this war. He is safe now. The government will never find him."

"I'm sorry Catherine, but I am glad to hear the child's safe." John replied, but he was very confused. John did not know what had happened since he went in seclusion; there was much to inform him of.

I could speak freely with John in the truck because we were surrounded by people we trusted. Sayid, Jacob, Peter, John and I were the only ones in this vehicle, save the driver and soldier in the passenger seat and they could not hear our conversation.

I was brief, but I told John all that had happened, "John, the plane did crash after I left Ireland, and although it is a matter of debate as to whether or not I actually died, I had a very vivid experience, that some have referred to as a, 'near death experience.' I went to Hell and then to Heaven. After meeting with God I was sent back to earth on a mission.

He equipped me with extra speed, agility, and strength. I am stronger and faster than an ordinary man and even than some demons. I regularly see both realms and pray in a version of Hebrew, even though I never spoke it before.

When I am moved to pray in this language miraculous things occur. It is as if I walk between two worlds, the spirit world and this world. I see both, I sense both and although I don't see the future, I have a sense or premonition about it.

Sky, whom you will meet this evening, calls me a Spirit Walker. The Lord who usually addresses me as child, and he has named me Timoshea in my visions."

John noted, "I believe it is a derivative of the Greek word Timotheos, meaning, 'honors God,' or he who honors God, Timoid is also an Irish name that means the same thing. Timoshe is a little different, maybe it means, she who honors God. Hmm, I've not studied Greek for many years, so I'm very rusty, but Shea is also an Irish name. I believe it means courageous and indomitable. That would loosely translate into, 'honors God with courage.' Sounds about right. Timoshea, that is a very unique name. You and I used to pour over both the original Greek and Hebrew writings in Ireland, remember. Sorry for interrupting please go on."

"I do remember, but you were the language expert. Anyways..." I continued, "...the world has been at war against a single dictator who has attempted to rule it. I believe it is Satan himself who has proclaimed himself God and who is attempting to rule the world. Satan calls himself Lumen and is using his puppet politician, General Augustus to achieve this."

Peter interjected, "I think this self-proclaimed god is simply an egomaniac who uses religion to manipulate the people, while the dictator Augustus uses an army to rule with an iron fist. This is not the first time in history this has happened, but Catherine believes it is the End Times as foretold in your bible."

Sayid added, "No matter what kind of evil we face, we fight against it, whether spiritual, or physical, or both. The world is still at war and Catherine is our leader in a movement against it. We fight to regain freedom and democracy and destroy the enemy.

We are on route to Jerusalem to free them from oppression and fight in what we agree is likely to be our final battle."

Peter added, "We are far apart on spiritual points of view, but we unite to fight the same enemy, and win our freedom. Some nations are divided with the rebels on one side and the political leaders on the other, but North America, Britain, Scotland, Ireland, Japan and Australia and what is left of France are finally unified in this mission. "

Peter looked a little sad for John as he continued to say, "So John," He sighed and then continued, "I don't know what you found in your mountains, or what peace and seclusion you have left behind, but where we go is into the heart of the conflict and it is going to be bloody and a battle from which we may not return. You have reentered society at the climax of the war.

Catherine is considered the most notorious of the rebel leaders and she is formidable. Although many rebels have succeed, she is the one the enemy most fears and hates.

You risk your very life being associated with her. You are more than welcome to join us, but you really don't strike me as the fighting type."

John chuckled, "I'm not, but even though I'm not a fighter, I would like to join you on your journey to Jerusalem. I can't explain it, but in my dreams I'm there and I am compelled to go. It is why I left the mountains to begin with. In my dreams I saw a great red Dragon. I saw the city of Jerusalem below and I was standing there with Catherine at the gates. I must be there."

Peter shook his head, "Are you going to risk your life for a dream?"

John smiled and said, "Yes, as are you."

Peter raised an eyebrow.

Sayid interjected, "We go because we dream of freedom and democracy; he goes because of a dream from God."

"Hmmm," Peter noted as he turned toward John, "Well if I recall you are a very good medic. Do you want to be the hands that heal?"

"I would." John replied

I added, "You can remain behind the lines and Sky will be with our unit on the battlefield. He is trained to fight if needed; he is our squad's medic now."

It was settled and I was glad that he was coming.

"Sargent Sayid," Peter addressed.

Sayid sat straighter. "Yes Captain." Sayid replied
Peter ordered, "No one off this truck can know Catherine's son is alive."

"Understood, Captain." Sayid responded.

I realized as we sat in silence that John was the only intimate friend I ever had. Peter knew me. Jacob knew me, but Jacob was my protector. He was kind of like a big brother, or uncle to me. Peter looked at me through the eyes of love, but I could not pray with him, I could not share my spiritual side with him, even though we loved each other completely, there was still a divide. Sayid shared my spiritual fervor, but he was still Muslim and I a Christian, so I could not walk in full faith with him either.

Spiritually I walked alone, but John had a unique and deep spiritual understanding of me as a person. John did not think me crazy when I discussed spiritual things and he did not judge me for my sensual side, while still holding me to account.

He did not view me as some great spiritual or military leader either; he was a good friend who accepted me as I am. He loved me and I loved him. I was thankful to have him back in my life.

I knew we both had changed and we could never go back to the way things were, I did not even know how he would fit into my new life, but I hoped it would all work out.

I will confess that I also hoped that he would help Peter have a deeper understanding of who God is.

I have never known anyone who understood God as profoundly as John. I knew God would reveal himself to Peter, but maybe he would use John in the process.

John and I had a soul tie that was so deep it was almost tangible and obvious to anyone who watched us.

I was amazed that even after all our years apart, we were still so deeply connected and so easy with each other.

Soul ties are not easily broken and being in Peter's arms and John's presence was strange, but in my spirit I was so glad to have my friend back in my life. He looked at me and I knew he was the only one next' to Jacob who saw me for who I really was.

*****

Chapter Six: United

We met up with Eric and made our way toward the ship. We shared a brotherhood and strength in our unity as we journeyed across the ocean toward Jerusalem. I had an uneasiness standing on the deck of the battleship and I had to ask Jacob, "Is this the final Battle?"

He answered me, "Oh Catherine, I like you long for peace. I hope the King will return soon and we shall enjoy a thousand years of earthly peace like never experienced before in history, but this will still be nothing compared to heaven.

Take comfort in being a soldier of the Almighty God; the battle will be bloody, but victory draws near. Many of us will die, but in death you shall rejoice in your everlasting life in the highest heaven and should you survive this battle, then you may yet enjoy the great honor of witnessing the return of the King of Heaven and Earth."

"So, you don't know either. Of course you don't. Only the Father knows." I noted with a sullen acceptance.

"Fear not Catherine. Trust in the Lord, for you are fighting the good fight spoken of in scripture; however you are correct, I do not know the future any more than you." Jacob said this as he placed an arm about me.

He could not answer my question. I was torn; I was thrilled I could finally marry Peter and then I was utterly dismayed as I remembered that Jesus said, "There is no marriage in heaven." Suddenly I was pained for I longed to be his wife and yet I was afraid that our union would be fleeting.

My whole focus was on the Lord and walking in the Spirit for so long that I had failed to make the most of what little time I would have with Peter. Life was so short. I had God with me always; I would be with him for eternity, but Peter and I had already lost so much time on earth. I made my way to my cabin as my emotional control diminished.

In my cabin I cried and I could not stop my tears from falling. Even though I found joy in the deep intimacy that I had with God, I needed more and I despised my foolishness in holding myself from Peter for so long. Now we were heading into what could result in our death and all this time I could have been his wife.

John came into my quarters and found me crying. I told him everything that I was feeling.

John said, "Catherine we must balance our spiritual lives and callings with our physical need for love. You were right, we are meant to be untied intimately with another human in the flesh and in the spirit as well. Let us pray to God and trust that it's not too late for love."

We bowed our head together and he held my hands and we prayed together John uttered these words, "Heavenly Father, Lord of mercy and grace, you are love, and we pray that you oh Lord give Catherine the opportunity to have that union, that intimacy that you intended from the beginning of creation. Bring forth for her a deep and beautiful marriage before she tastes death. Bless her with the love that you intended.

I praise you for bringing her back into my life Lord and I trust that you will grant both her and Peter a long and fruitful life. Amen."

We were holding hands in prayer and I was still crying and John was wiping my tears away when Peter walked in the room. He said, "Catherine, are you okay?"

I got up and assured him, "I'm fine."

He glanced at John, and then Peter wiped the tears from my face and questioned, "Then tell me, why you're crying?"

"Forgive me Peter; I wasted so much precious time. I should have married you long ago. We lost so much time and life is short. I was a fool forgive me." My voice quivered and the tears flowed once again.

Peter sighed with relief and spoke gently to me, "It is alright my dear, sweet, Catherine. We'll marry now, right now. I just spoke to the Chaplin you are about to become my wife."

I kissed him and then I turned and hugged and kissed John too. I asked, "When's the ceremony?"

"Tonight at 18:00 hours, there are a few guests who are joining us from other ships; one insisted that we wait for him." Peter replied with a little grin, "He insisted that we wait, and he has a special gift for you. He'll be landing in two hours."

"Peter" I warned, "It is not a good way to start a marriage by keeping secrets, who is it?"

He chided, "We aren't married yet." Then he kissed my cheek and assured me, "I am sure this will be the only secret that I keep from you my love. I will leave you to get ready; I have other things to attend to."

With that he turned and left before I could ask, "What things?" Peter had already made his way out the door whistling a tune so that he could pretend not to hear me.

I turned back to look at John, and I hugged him and he kissed my cheek and excused himself by saying, "Congratulations Catherine, I will leave you to get ready."

I hugged him again and expressed my gratitude, "Thank you John, I'm so glad you're here with me, to share the happiest day of my life."

"Me too." He replied and then he kissed me again and turned to walk out the door.

I didn't know how I would prepare myself, all I had was my combat clothes, but I thought aloud, "Don't be silly. It doesn't matter what you wear, all that matters is you get to marry the man you love." I decided the least I could do was shower and then there was a knock at the door.

Jacob came in and notified me, "A sailor delivered this to you and said it was a gift for the wedding ceremony and he said that you should open it and use it right away."

I opened the black bag and inside was a razor, shaving cream, body lotion, shampoo and conditioner. I asked, "Who is it from?"

Jacob cleared his throat and answered sheepishly, "Sayid sent it, but he did not deliver it himself in case... just in case it offended you. The young lieutenant informed me that Sayid thought you would not like to be hairy and smelly like a man on your wedding night, but be more like..." Jacob paused and then continued, "...like a woman."

I laughed and then said, "I will thank him later." I washed up and then I asked Jacob to bring the shampoo and conditioner to Peter to use as well, I ordered, "Tell Sayid to give it to Peter. I want him to have soft, silky hair too."

I made my way up the stairs. I stood upon the deck staring into the sea, thankful that I would be with the man I loved and then my thoughts went to my son. I wondered how he was doing and if he missed me as much as I missed him. I was a little forlorn and Jacob joined me and he commented, "He misses you too Catherine, but he is enjoying his life."

"I thought you couldn't read minds." I mused

Jacob smiled and acknowledged, "I can't, but I can read you. I know you; you have been in my charge since you were born."

Jacob took my hands in his and warned, "Before you make your vows there are something I must warn you about."

I looked concerned, but I said nothing as Jacob continued, "Your powers are growing and they will continue to develop. You are a half breed Catherine and you have crossed over to the other side. I do not know how long you will be given in this realm before..."

I finished Jacob's sentence, "Before the angels are ordered to hunt me down."

Jacob sighed, "I don't know what will become of you Catherine, but I lived through the Nephilim reign of Terror before. God will not allow such a thing to happen again. Before the rise of the Nephilim, he will intervene."

I smiled and assured Jacob, "He already has Jacob. I am not the only one, there are more. Satan changed the direction of the war. Don't worry, I don't know everything, but I know my destiny. My powers are ordained by God himself. My son and others like me will battle with the angels, alongside the warriors of men and we will defeat the Devil and his armies."

Jacob's temperament did not change as he added, "Catherine, I am confident we will win, but that does not mean we will not be sacrificed. The balance must be restored and if you do survive, I would be surprised if you were not made barren."

I was puzzled as I inquired, "Jacob what has got into you? You are not one for conjecture. What do you know?"

"I don't know anything for sure, but I have this sense of foreboding, that is growing within me."

Jacob continued, "I also need to warn you that as your powers grow so will your senses and your emotional responses will become amplified. You must learn restraint and self-control or Heaven will be called down to put an end to you and your kind. It happened before and I fear it will again. I am designed to protect you, but you must ensure you do not succumb to the darkness within you."

"Wow, you are just full of cheer today. Don't worry Jacob I've seen Heaven and Hell and I will never cross over to the dark side. Don't worry, all will be okay." I tried to assure him, but my words had little effect, so I asked him, "Jacob, do you trust God?"

"Yes." Jacob answered.

"Well he chose me and he chose John, don't you think God knows what he is doing?"

Jacob looked melancholy as he replied, "He also made man and he chose Satan before the fall. Satan was the most beautiful, powerful and trusted among all of God's creation. He was second only to God Catherine and we angels were not granted the luxury of free will. We are designed to obey. You have a human soul married with the attributes of the Divine. It is a dangerously overwhelming combination."

"Jacob, Satan is among the first of the angelic beings and you are very young compared to him. Perhaps you are designed to obey, but other orders of angelic hosts were not. Have you thought of that?" I challenged.

"No, and you may be correct, but it does not change a thing. Heed my warning, please. You have no idea the depth of the dark power that flows through your veins." Jacob pleaded.

I took Jacob's arm and we turned to walk away, "I will be on guard Jacob, I promise and if I falter, I give you permission to kick my ass and protect me from myself."

Jacob responded solemnly, "That's the problem Catherine, should you falter, I will not have the power to. Angels older and greater then I will be ordered to."

"I won't fall from grace. I promise." I assured him.

Then, when we noticed a fighter jet landing on the aircraft carrier parallel to us we stood silently watching. We could not make out who it was, but they got on a helicopter and made their way to our ship. I was glad I had braided my hair because it would have been a mess had I not.

I laughed out loud as I recognized Yuri instantly. The chopper returned to the other vessel and I said, "Yuri, I am so glad to see you. Are you the one Peter told me to wait for?"

He kissed both my cheeks and he said, "Yes, I hear you are getting married and I could not let you celebrate such a wonderful occasion without me. Now tell me little lady, what are you planning to wear?"

I motioned to the clothes I was wearing, "Yes, we feared as much. Bourbon could not be here in time, he will meet us in Hawaii. He is on route, but he insisted I get you a beautiful dress to wear,"

Vladimir, one of Yuri's body guards gave me a box, Jacob held it for me while I opened it to peek inside. I gasped, "It is beautiful Yuri. Thank you."

"You are welcome, but it was Bourbon's idea." Yuri smiled and added, "I picked it though, it is sexy, but tasteful. Now go get ready, the wedding is only few hours away."

I was shocked as I said, "A few hours, how long do you think it will take me?"

Sayid joined us on deck and he shook Yuri's hand and chimed in, "That is what I feared, how long did it take you to clean yourself up? Yuri, we're glad you could make it."

I noticed Sayid had the black bag in his hand again and he said, "Did you read the directions on the conditioner bottle? Of course you didn't, you are supposed to leave this in for at least twenty minutes before rinsing."

I glared at Sayid a little and said, "Since when did the navy seal become an expert on hair care."

"Very funny; since I married a woman and Yuri has another surprise for you."

"What?" I inquired as another plane landed on the aircraft carrier beside us. Two people were escorted onto the chopper and were transported to our ship. Yuri helped two beautiful women get off the chopper. They both wore black dresses and red high heel shoes.

After it flew away Yuri introduced, Katrina and Tanya to me. He kissed their hands and I offered my hand to them and shook theirs as I said, "Hello"

Yuri cleared his throat and said, "These two beautiful ladies are going to help you get ready for your wedding."

"What makes you think I need help? I don't need help." I insisted.

Tanya said in a thick Russian accent, "Your comrades feel you may have forgotten how to be like woman. From the coarseness of your hands I fear, you will need both of us to help you."

"You are, how do you say it?" Katrina searched for the right words.

Sayid finished her sentence, "...more like one of the guys."

I hit Sayid with an elbow to his gut and he bent over and said, "Thank you for proving our point."

Yuri took both my hands and said, "You are very beautiful Catherine, no one would dispute that. I have never met a more gorgeous and amazing woman than you, but you have lived with soldiers for too long.

You have become accustomed to a warriors way of life, and we all love and admire you for that, but today is your wedding day and we all want it to be perfect for you. Please let us help you?"

John joined us on deck and he put his arm around me and said, "Catherine you made me shave and clean up as soon as possible when you found me on that road, now it's your turn. Common be good and let everyone help you."

I laughed remembering what John looked like when I picked him up and then I said, "I don't look that bad, do I?"

John kissed my cheek and said, "You could never look that bad, beautiful."

"Alright" I sighed, "Let's get this over with." I caved to the pressure and made my way below decks as Jacob, Sayid and the women with two suitcases of supplies followed me to my cabin.

Jacob and Sayid left us and Tanya gave me shorts and a T-shirt to wear. Then the women began to work on me.

I could not help, but admire Tanya with her long soft chestnut hair and sultry brown eyes and Katrina with her shoulder length layered black hair and brown eyes. They both had a beautiful shade of red lipstick and long red nails.

I was aware as soon as I shook their hands how soft their skin was and how rough and calloused mine were. Oh well, mountain climbing is hard work. You cannot be a fighter and a lady, but for one day I would try.

Katrina suggested, "Let us start with your hair; it looks like it has been years since you had it cut."

I remarked, "It has, since before the war."

Tanya pondered and sighed "Well, wet it down and then we will give you long layers, everyone wears their hair up for their wedding day, but men like it down."

Katrina said, "Yes, but it is very alluring when you wear up and then let it down just before you make love."

Tanya mused, "This is very true." Then she asked me, "What would you prefer?"

I didn't like people touching my hair, so I replied, "Whatever's quicker and I need to be able to easily tie it back for the battlefield."

They looked at one another and both declared, "Down."

Katrina began to cut my hair and then she commented, "This is very good decision, for we have much work to do."

I did not reply as they worked on me, I couldn't anyway for they placed a whitening mouth guard in my mouth while they worked and put some kind of mask on my face. It was green. I must have looked ridiculous.

After the hair cut they washed my face and then my hair again, followed by the conditioner. They left it in for about thirty minutes while they gave me a simultaneous pedicure and manicure. They rinsed my hair; they blow dried it and styled it with log soft curls.

Then they stuck both my hands and feet in paraffin wax. Then they heated wax stripes and ripped the hair follicles from my arms and legs, I questioned, "Do we really have to do this? I already shaved."

Tanya answered, "Yes, we must; it would have worked better if you didn't shave, but it will still give you very soft skin."

Then they were about to tweeze my eyebrows, when I said, "I don't like pencil thin eyebrows, I like them the way they are."

I was firm, but both women were not phased and Tanya boldly stated, "Your eye brows are bushy; we will simply clean them up a bit."

I cautioned them, "Don't make them too thin."

They replied, "Trust us we will make you beautiful."

Trust did not come easily to me and I was not used to people disregarding my orders and then they began to apply my makeup. I warned them, "I don't wear make-up and I don't like a lot of it, I don't want to look like a made up doll, I could lose the men's respect."

"Tovarisch" Katrina uttered more like a swear word then what it actually meant, 'comrade or friend.'

She continued only mildly exasperated with her hands on her hips as she questioned, "Do you think we are beautiful?"

I answered, "You are both breathtaking."

Katrina said, "Spa-see-ba," meaning thank you in Russian and then she said, "We do each other's, hair and nails all the time and sometimes each other's make up too. Please do not be so difficult. Trust us."

Tanya added, "Besides you are already beautiful and a brave warrior, looking gorgeous will not lose your men's' respect it will only deepen their love, and commitment to you. After we are through with you there is nothing they would not do for you. Trust us, please."

I nodded and gave them free reign. It took what felt like an eternity to finish. Finally they applied fake nails and decorated them with red and a single diamond like stone on each nail. After my nails dried I changed into my dress and they tied the back bodice up.

They both commented, "You are beautiful Catherine"

"Thank you both. I appreciate all you have done." I replied sincerely as I looked in the mirror.

They both smiled and said, "Pa-zhal-sta" meaning your welcome.

Jacob knocked on the door, "It is time; are you ready?"

"Nyet, no, no." Tanya said, "You need something borrowed, something blue, something old and something new, yes?"

I smiled and then said, "Well, everything I am wearing is new."

Katrina took a beautiful hair comb from her own hair made from white pearls and put my hair slightly up on one side and declared, "Something borrowed."

Then they both frowned as Yuri came in through the door and declared, "Something blue." He smiled as he placed a beautiful sapphire and diamond bracelet on my right wrist.

I touched it and said, "Yuri this is beautiful, but it is all too much."

Yuri kissed my hand and said, "Don't be silly; it is also very old and blue. It was owned and worn by Catherine the Great."

I gasped, "Yuri how did you get your hands on this?"

Yuri smiled, "I have many people indebted to me. Now come, it is time. Are you ready?"

"Yes, she is." Tanya answered for me. Tanya and Katrina had also changed into beautiful red dresses while my nails were drying, so we were all dressed beautifully for my wedding.

I took Jacob's arm and he led me to the mess hall, however when we arrived it looked nothing like one. I don't know how they did it, but there was a red carpet down the center of the room. The tables where all covered with white linens and there were red carnations with babies breath on every table.

Everyone who was former military was dressed in their formal military uniforms. A military band played as John brought me a bouquet of red carnations with white babies' breath and green ferns.

In the middle of the bouquet was a single red rose and a single white rose. It was beautiful and much like the one Peter had delivered to me many years before when he left Ireland.

I cried and John kissed my cheek and caressed my face as he wiped away my tears and warned,

"You are so beautiful. Now don't cry Catherine, you'll mess up your lovely makeup."

I laughed and then Katrina whispered, "Don't worry; it is waterproof."

I smiled and then I asked, "John, Will you walk me down the aisle?"

John gave me his arm and answered, "I would be honored."

I made my way to the front of the room holding my bouquet in one arm and holding onto John with the other. Everyone stood as I made my way up the aisle.

I felt somewhat uncomfortable as every eye admired my long, white, shimmering satin dress. The bodice was form fitting and it was laced up the back with beautiful white and silver ribbon. The bottom flowed gently as I walked down the aisle.

Peter stood at the front looking breathtaking in his uniform with Sayid beside him. John walked up and stood to my left.

The Chaplin read some traditional marriage scriptures and then Peter said the vows he wrote for me.

Peter took my hands after I handed John my flowers to hold and Peter declared, "Catherine Miles, I love you. I love you more than life itself. You captured my heart in Ireland. I publicly declare before all who stand here today that I will always be, loyal and faithful and wholly devoted to you and you alone. I will be your husband, I will honor you, I will respect you and I will support and protect you as long as I live."

He wiped the tear falling down my cheek and I smiled. I spoke softly as he held my hand tenderly in his and I returned my vows, "Peter Joseph Roberts' today in front of God and man, I publicly declare my love for you. I give myself to you as your wife. Long have you had my heart and today I give you my hand in marriage. I promise that I will be faithful to you, love you and stand by you, protecting you, respecting you and honoring you above all others, being wholly devoted to you as long as I live."

It came time to exchange rings and then music began and I saw my son John walking into the room with two rings tide to a white satin pillow. Lazaro and Nahor were on either side of him as he walked up to meet us. I knelt down, so did Peter and we each took a ring, I hugged and kissed John and caressed his face.

Then I turned and faced Peter. We placed our wedding bands on each other. We and our witnesses signed the registry and license.

The preacher then declared, "I now present to you Peter and Catherine Roberts, husband and wife. You may kiss the bride." Peter kissed me passionately and then he whispered, "I love you Mrs. Roberts."

I smiled and I replied, "I love you too." Everyone cheered.

It was not long when Lazaro whispered in my ear, "We cannot stay Catherine. We must get Raziel away from here as soon as possible. His very presence with you invites danger."

I knelt down and hugged my son again and I said, "I love you John. Be strong, and learn well. I am going to miss you."

He kissed my cheek and whispered, "I am going to miss you too Mommy, but I am glad I got to see you marry Peter. Don't worry I am having a wonderful time. I wish you could come with me Mommy, you would love it too. I was warned that we could not stay long and I want this day to be happy for you, so don't cry okay."

"Okay John, I love you." We both spoke softly so that no one could hear us. Some knew I had a baby, but few knew how quickly he was growing, so they did not suspect that he was my son. Even though he had my blue eyes his hair was a very blond and long, like Nahor and his features were different from my own.

I noticed Yuri approaching so I shook Lazaro and Nahor's hand as I said, "Thank you all for coming, we both appreciate you attending. Good-bye. I'm sorry you couldn't stay longer."

Lazaro replied, "We were happy to attend and we all wish you both the best."

Peter shook each of their hands including John's and said, "Thank you for coming and for your help, you did a great job."

"Thank you for having us Peter." Nahor replied and then all three bowed to us and left.

Yuri boisterously said, "Congratulations you two. I am so happy for you, now we must drink and celebrate. I have brought the finest Russian vodka. Let the celebration begin."

The band began to play and Peter bowed and requested, "Mrs. Roberts, may I have this dance?"

I curtsied and we laughed and then he took me in his arms and as we swayed to the music I said, "You are full of surprises. How did you manage to set this entire thing up in time?"

"I had a lot of friends help out. Everybody loves you Catherine and we all wanted this to be an incredible day for you." Peter responded.

"Well you all did an amazing job. It's beautiful." I looked about the room I could not believe how this all came together on a battleship.

He caressed my cheek and countered, "You are beautiful."

He tilted my chin toward him and I kissed him again. We continued our dance and I inquired, "How did you get John here?"

"Jacob" Peter replied.

"You're all amazing. I am so blessed to have you. Where did you find the flowers?" I asked.

Peter tilted his head and smiled as he looked at our Russian friends enjoying Russian vodka as he said, "I contacted Yuri and had him bring them."

"Wow, you thought of everything. The bouquet you gave me is like the one in Ireland." I remarked.

Peter smiled his gorgeous smile and whispered, "Yes, I added a red rose to symbolize the passion we share and a white rose to honor the purity you retained in waiting to surrender to me. You lived up to the meaning of your name after all."

"Only in deed Peter." I laughed and then I whispered, "If you knew the thoughts I have had all of these years about you, you would be shocked and you would see that I really don't deserve the name, but I love the flowers. They're beautiful."

"Thus the reason for the red rose my dear Catherine, and you can tell me and show me every passionate fantasy you have had while we will live them out together. Let's begin now." Peter replied as he led me away from the dance floor.

Yuri was dancing with his two beautiful ladies and waved goodbye to us as we made our way to our cabin. We would rarely leave our cabin for the rest of the journey except to eat and share a stroll on deck. One night after making love to him I said, "This is the closest thing to heaven on earth I have found."

Peter laughed out loud and I added, "I have a new favorite scripture."

He took me in his arms and he questioned, "What scripture is that?"

I smiled quoted, "The two shall become one."

Peter grinned as he replied, "I am kind of partial to that one myself." Then he kissed me again.

The honeymoon was bliss, and then Jacob knocked on the cabin door and announced the ship was docking in Hawaii.

Peter and I went and found a beach and went swimming. Hawaii was the most beautiful place I had ever been in my life. It took my breath away. I wished I could stay here with Peter forever. It was as if the war never even touched this paradise.

When we returned to the ship we had joined our friends in the mess hall and we joined up for a feast with all of the other rebel leaders. The first to greet us was Hideki Yamamoto; he bowed and then kissed my hand and said, "Congratulations. We are all very happy for you two."

I responded, "Thank you that is very kind of you, Hideki."

"I have a gift for both of you." His body guard passed me a black box with red writing on it. Hideki told me, "It reads, 'Meiyo to seigi no tame no' that is, 'For honor and justice' in Japanese. I hope you both enjoy them."

I opened the box and it was filled with beautiful throwing knives, eight in all. Each blade had different Japanese symbols on them. Hideki read them for us, "They read, 'yuuki, meyio, yuu, seishinryoku, seigō, kōhei, chūsei, masayoshi,' they mean, 'courage, honor, valor, strength, integrity, impartiality, allegiance, and justice.' I felt that both of you demonstrate all of these qualities."

I kissed Hideki on the cheek and said, "Domo arigato," meaning, 'Thank you." I admired them for a moment and then I added, "They're beautiful and I am honored.'

Bourbon was there and he brought us two gifts, "Bonjour Madam, you look beautiful. I am so glad

Eric took pictures, he just finished showing us them. You were absolutely divine."

"Merci beaucoup Monsieur le President." I replied in French.

"Catherine, please call me Louis." Bourbon insisted.

"Louis, I thought your first name was Charles." Peter queried.

"Oh, oui, oui, yes, yes, it is, but my full name is, Charles Louis Bourbon. My friends and family call me Louis." He explained.

"Louis suits you Bourbon." Yuri noted as he raised his vodka in a toast and drank.

"My dear friends I too have a couple of gifts for you." Louis announced as he waved to his body guards who passed each of us a gift.

Peter opened a huge box full of chocolate truffles and assorted chocolates from France and I received a box full of several bottles of Merlot.

"Louis," Peter noted, "These are wonderful gifts, I believe we should share them tonight."

"C'est une bonne idée, what a wonderful idea Peter, I agree." Bourbon was only too happy to partake with us in such pleasures.

I kissed Bourbon on the cheek and said, "Mercie, Thank you Louis; you remembered my favorite wine. You have exquisite taste."

Yuri said, "Where is my kiss? I brought the dress and flowers remember."

I walked around the table and kissed his cheek as well and Yuri said, "Ahh, Peter you are a lucky man."

Peter put his arms around my waist and agreed, "Yes I am, Yuri." Peter pulled out a chair for me and we all sat down and tasted the chocolate.

It was the most wonderful chocolate I had ever eaten. We all complimented Louis who raised his glass of wine to us and said, "To the most amazing and beautiful couple I've ever met. May your light and love burn bright and bring you much joy for many years to come and to us all being together again."

"Here, here." Yuri chimed and we all drank and feasted together. Sky joined us as well. Sayid did not drink, but he enjoyed the camaraderie.

John came in and I introduced him to everyone. I announced, "Everyone I would like to introduce you to my oldest and beloved friend, John."

John waved and said, "Hello everyone."

"Hello" They all replied in unison

"John I would like to introduce you to some of the most notorious rebel leaders in the world. To my left is Hideki Yamamoto, beside him is Yuri Sasha Michaelovich, and to his left is Charles Louis Bourbon. You already know Sayid, Sky and Eric." John nodded

Yuri insisted, "Please sit and join us; we are celebrating the union of our two friends here. Drink, would you like some good Russian Vodka, or fine French Merlot?"

"Actually, I prefer some ice cold Canadian beer, do you have any?" John inquired.

"Ah, Canadian beer is very good, but weak. You Canadians do not know how to drink. We Russians are the best drinkers in the world. There is nothing better than real Russian vodka." Yuri declared proudly

A Scottish sailor at the table next to us said, "I beg your pardon, but I must protest. We Scotts are the best drinkers. Russian vodka is very good, but we invented Scotch whisky. There is nothing like it. We Scotts hold our liquor very well. We go to a pub almost every night in Scotland."

"Nonsense boy, we Russians consume absinth, have you heard of it? It is 180 proof. We mix that with your energy drinks and have them for breakfast." Yuri retorted.

"Drink too much of that and it will kill you." Peter warned.

"Ah, yes this is true, but we Russians are very strong. You all mix your fruity drinks and sip your wine, but we, we drink straight vodka, no mix."

Louis observed, "You drink to get drunk, mon ami, however my friend, we French drink to please the palate."

Yuri said, "This is true, we drink to forget the cold and warm the body. Do you know how cold it gets in Russia and how long the winter lasts in Moscow? It is very harsh, but it makes us very strong and vodka makes us very happy."

The young Scott stood up and said, "Well growing up in Scotland is no picnic, either. It is damp and cold every day and there is nothing like a damp cold to test a man's fortitude. We should see and find out, who is the better man? I challenge you to a drinking contest."

Sky cautioned, "Don't be foolish Petty Officer Craig, you could get alcohol poisoning from either whisky or vodka."

"I have had many drinking games and never once has it hurt me." Yuri replied.

"Aye, me neither. So are we on?" The Scot challenged.

Sky said, "This is foolish, but please drink water before and after as well as take an aspirin before you turn in."

"Aye." The Scott replied.

We sat back as bottle of Scottish whisky and a bottle of Russian vodka were both placed on the table and the shot glasses were brought as well. Yuri said, "Well Private Craig, we'll take one shot of vodka, followed by one shot of whisky and see which one of us is the better man."

"It sounds fair to me, Commander Michaelovich." Craig replied.

The Petty Officer's friends surrounded him and one shouted, "Common Dougie boy, show em what you're made of."

Yuri laughed, "Doggy, is that your nick name?"

"No, not Doggy, they call my Dougie as short for Douglas. Ahh, let's drink."

They had both already had a few too many and I did not think the game could take too long. I was wrong. We watched as each of them had nine rounds and the men cheered their champion on. Then on the tenth the boy got ill. It was not a pretty sight his mates helped him to his room.

I am sure Yuri would soon be ill as well, but he maintained his composure and only looked a little drunk as he retired for the evening, with the help of both Tanya and Katrina and Yuri exclaimed, "The only thing better than vodka to keep you warm in Russia is a good Russian woman, or two." The ladies laughed as the led Yuri from the mess hall.

The next morning Peter and Sky went to check on the boy, he was very ill indeed. The second day the boy was barely ready to eat breakfast and Peter said, "There are three things you should learn from this son. One, never mix your alcohols especially hard liquor. Two, listen to advice and drink a lot of water and take your aspirin next time. Three, never challenge someone to a drinking game that has at least two decades of drinking tolerance on you, especially a Russian." Peter patted his shoulder and made his way to our table.

I stopped and said, "Sky will be bringing you some bitters; take them, it will ease your suffering." He said nothing, but nodded and I joined Peter for breakfast.

Sayid stopped as well and added, "The best advice son is to never drink at all. We Muslims don't consume alcohol."

The boy grimaced and replied, "Mohammed was a wise man, thank you sir."

Sayid patted his shoulder and joined us. Eric, John and the rebel leaders were already seated and they were having breakfast. Peter brought me a coffee and eggs and toast.

"Mmm, I'm craving Eggs Benedict. I have not had that in so long." I mused aloud

Bourbon heard me and said, "What a wonderful idea."

He waved to his servant and whispered in his ear and then ordered, "Take this away, we will all enjoy eggs Benedict, it has been far too long since I enjoyed them too."

The servant complied and began to take our plates away save Sayid who said, "My meal is fine thank you."

Bourbon pleaded, "Please forgive me Sayid, no offense intended. You see, I have no such dietary restrictions. Je suis désolé."

"There is nothing to forgive, President Bourbon, no offence was taken."

Yuri asked, "How is the boy doing?"

I answered, "He'll be okay, but I think he regrets the challenge."

"Yes, but we must all live and hopefully learn from our mistakes." Yuri laughed.

"I don't think he will be repeating that mistake again." Sayid declared.

I chastised Yuri a little and commented, "Yuri you knew the boy couldn't win, you shouldn't of accepted the challenge."

Peter said, "My love, Yuri's right, some lessons have to be lived to be learned, and the boy had to be humbled."

I frowned and then I said, "I suppose, but I feel for him."

Yuri noted, "That is because you are a woman Catherine, but don't mother the boy, we are simply helping him learn some hard lessons on his journey to become a man."

I looked at Sayid and said, "See Sayid, it is because I am a woman. Did you hear that?"

Sayid raised his hands and retorted, "Okay, ease up. Doesn't your holy book say, forgive and forget?"

"No Sayid, it commands forgive and I forgive you, but nowhere do I recall forget." I replied.

Yuri patted Peter's back and said, "Be careful my friend, a woman never forgets. It is best you learn this now, so that you can ensure you are never in the dog house like poor Sayid here." Everyone laughed in unison.

******

Chapter Seven: The Eye of the Storm

We enjoyed our breakfast and then we went to train. Yamomoto was practicing the way of the Samurai with his men. I was fighting against Peter practicing sword play as well and Hideki approached me and pleaded, "May I suggest something to you both?"

I insisted, "Please do."

"I know that you are both exceptional warriors and few mortals can compare to you, but should we fight men as large as Jacob, your American-European style of hand to hand combat will not suffice, Captain." He bowed a humbly and continued, "May I demonstrate?"

"Of course." Peter answered.

"Europeans often fight with the sword like this..." Hideki held his sword above his head and struck in strong long swings. "The strike is deliberate and deadly, but it is a separate motion from defense." He said, "The sword play for them is dependent upon the wielders strength and speed, however because each move has a beginning and an end; there is a moment in between each motion, thereby giving your assailant time to strike."

He then demonstrated the Japanese form and said, "However a Samurai fights with the sword as an extension of his own body and soul. It is a fluid motion, allowing one movement to flow seamlessly into the next. It depends on speed, agility and awareness, all qualities you both share."

He showed us the concept again and ordered, "You two try." Peter and I practiced and then Soku took Peter as a partner and Kato took me as one, while Hideki corrected and guided us. We practiced for hours every day as we journeyed toward Jerusalem.

We progressed quickly and thanked Hideki with a bow, before and after each training session. He had become our own personal sensei. At the end of each session we meditated.

He also taught us the art of throwing our knives and showed us the best places to wear them on our bodies.

One day during hand to hand combat he asked Peter, "Peter do you know why it is that a little woman, like Catherine, or a smaller man like Soku defeats you?"

Peter answered, "Because they are faster and more agile than I. They also transfer their entire force to single points of contact."

"Yes, but they also use the larger and stronger opponents force and momentum against them. They do not try to block a stronger strike directly, as much as they direct it away while absorbing some of its force. It is similar to the sword play. Strike me and I will block like you." Hideki ordered and Peter complied.

Yamomoto continued, "As men we can often get away with such a style of fighting, but when our opponent is much larger, like Jacob. We must direct that force like a dance. I will show you first with a punch and then with a sword. Jacob, will you strike me?"

Jacob bowed and complied, Hideki rather than blocking the punch, side stepped while directing the punch away from the path it was taking.

Peter observed, "Yes I see it, this style is like a combination of Kung-fu and Karate. It is fluid rather than abrupt."

"Very good Peter, you are a quick learner. Practice against Jacob and Yuri's men and you will be better prepared to face Augustus's soldiers.

Hideki nodded and proceeded to practice his own techniques himself as Peter began to spar with Vladimir while Jacob and I fought with each other.

Applying the same philosophy of movement to our hand to hand combat and our swards made us even better fighters.

One day Hideki advised, "When the modern weapons of warfare fail to be useful, or they are not available, a warrior will fight by other means. Always be prepared for every kind of battle, but you are likely to only be a true master of one.

Your people say, 'don't be a jack of all trades and a master of none.' This is wise advice, but knowledge is power, so be familiar with more than one way of fighting. Peter I think you were born to be a master swordsman, you have the spirit of a samurai warrior."

Peter bowed and smiled, "Thank you Hideki, I am honored and will I practice what you've taught me, but I am far more comfortable with a gun at my side. I think I will put my faith in my skills with a gun before I trust in my sword."

Yuri agreed, "Yes I love my, semi-automatic pistols, I am never without them and a nice machine gun is very good too."

Peter smiled, "I agree Yuri, I don't leave home without mine either."

Soku interjected and said, "We agree Captain, but a warrior must be prepared for a day when all other weapons fail."

Yuri said, "Da, Yes, yes and we have all trained hard, and we are ready. You are all ready to be like ninja. Let's eat."

Kato corrected Yuri, "Commander Michailovich we are not ninja. They practice the dark arts."

Hideki added, "We are decedents of an ancient and Nobel bloodline that fights by the Light of the Bushido Code. A ninja is not moral and they fight for anyone who pays them enough. They have no honor."

Yuri bowed to Hideki and then the other Japanese warriors and apologized, "Please forgive me comrade, I did not know. I did not intend to offend you."

Hideki bowed back and replied, "Pinapatawad kita, I forgive you Yuri."

"Dude..." Eric smirked, "How old are you? Now-a-days Ninjas are epic."

We all laughed for only Eric could get away with such a comment to Commander Hideki. We made our way to shower in silence as Eric said, "What...its true haven't you ever heard someone say, 'That's totally Ninja?'"

Hideki replied, "No, I have not and my age is not a sign of being out of touch, rather your age and saying is a reflection of your generation's ignorance. If you saw a true ninja warrior, you would be staring into the eyes of evil Eric son."

"Forgive me Commander Hideki, I meant no offence."

"None taken, when we learn truth only then can we speak without ignorance. A wise man takes correction and does not repeat the mistake again. Only when he continues to utter such things once he has learned not to, is offence taken." Hideki schooled.

"I won't ever say such a thing again, I promise." Eric swore with sincerity and then we proceeded to the showers and then back to the mess-hall to eat.

At supper that evening John was engaged in a conversation with Sayid when we arrived. John questioned, "Sayid, how are you as a Muslim able to go and kill those from your homeland in the coming battle? Aren't you forbidden from killing your brethren?"

"Yes, like Christians and Jews we are forbidden from committing murder against our brothers and sisters of the faith and we are forbidden to murder people of the book who worship the one true God."

John interjected, "Then how do you rationalize all the jihadists who have killed Jews, and the terrorists, who killed Christians for several decades now?"

"John, they are gravely deceived, they think they are going to paradise for murdering these innocent people and committing suicide, but both are not the Muslim way. Mohammed would never condone it. Allah will punish all of these terrorists and suicide bombers with eternal fire; the Qur'an reads, 'Allah judges with integrity'

John nodded and declared, "How do you then rationalize killing the people of your culture and religion, in the coming battle?"

"John, the people I fight against cannot be true Muslims. If they are trying to annihilate anyone who worships the one true God they are not true Muslims, if they support Augustus and Lumen the self-proclaimed god, who is not god, they are not true Muslims. The Qur'an says, 'Should any of you desert his religion, Allah will soon bring a people whom He loves and whom love Him, who will be humble towards the faithful, stern toward the faithless, waging jihad in the way of Allah.' Jihad is reserved for holy war against the enemies of God and those who have betrayed him. Many of my brothers have waged jihad already against Lumen and Augustus. I shall not be killing them. We may also engage in war against the infidel and kill the nonbelievers should they stand against Islam."

Peter interjected and questioned, "Sayid, I am an infidel according to your book, would you kill me?"

Sayid smiled, "Roberts, I will be forgiven for doing so, but it does not mean I should or that I must, so you are safe for now my friend. Besides you are a Deist and closer to the faith than you know. "

Then John questioned Sayid again, "I'm sorry; I am only curious. I don't intend to cause any ill will or question your faith Sayid, but I must ask you this, you consider Peter and Catherine and Eric your friends, do you not?"

"Yes I do, I would sacrifice my life to protect any of them." Sayid answered honestly.

John then said, "Well, doesn't your Qur'an forbid that?"

Sayid replied, "Yes it reads, 'O you who have faith! Do not take those who take your religion in derision and play, from among those who were given the Book before you and the infidels, as friends and be wary'

This is a warning, like your book of proverbs, it is words of wisdom. If I am surrounded by people who lack in faith and morals, I am liable to be corrupted, tempted to sin. Your bible warns of something similar. It is suggested to not surround your-selves with those who drink, carouse and engage in sin openly, have nothing to do with them at all, I believe it suggests this. In fact your bible warns, 'Do not be unequally yoked with a non-believer.' Does it not?"

John responded, "Yes, because it is hard enough to be faithful to God and walk in the faith, but to do so when the one you love and your friends do not share your walk, means you walk alone. It is a difficult spiritual journey. They may even lead us away from the faith as Solomon's wives did. Isn't it forbidden for a Muslim to marry a non-believer and yet you did; can you explain this?"

Sayid smiled, "In General John, Muslim men are not permitted to marry non-Muslim women in many of the extreme religious sects. They are not totally wrong for the Qur'an reads, 'Do not marry unbelieving women until they believe... Unbelievers beckon you to the Fire.' However they miss the great Mercy and grace of Allah, for an exception is made for Muslim men to marry a pure or moral woman, who worships the one God. They are referred to as 'People of the Book.' Allah is indeed our one God brother."

John questioned, "But she is still considered a non-believer?"

Sayid nodded, "Yes, It is very similar for us as between you Catholics and Protestants. Both of you believe Jesus is Messiah, the Christ, but your doctrines vary. I married my wife, a Christian, because I loved her. Peter here does not believe as Catherine believes and yet he stole her heart too. However Allah is merciful and gracious and we are weak, especially when it comes to matters of the heart."

John said, "I understand, but how do you Sayid and any of you condone killing? How can you have faith in the Merciful God and go to war at all?"

"This is a difficult task John, none of us here embrace war; we long for peace, but we are soldiers. If anyone, no matter their religion, creed or culture attacks the United States, threatens our freedom, or even threatens to kill Americans, I will willingly kill them without remorse.

As for Jerusalem, the city that is under siege is not the city of the Jew, the Christian or the Muslim. It is, Alhamdulillah, Praise God, a city for all of mankind. It belongs to no one and all three major faiths reside within her city walls. I go to free the people, not fight for a religion." Sayid declared.

John shook his head as said, "I could not kill; I could not fight as you do."

Yuri patted his back and said, "John that is because you are not a warrior, and we fight in your stead. You pray we succeed."

I corrected Yuri, "Oh John is a warrior, a prayer warrior. We may fight with our hands, but he fights on his knees."

"This is true and you and Sayid appear to be both. Well, we are sure to succeed then. It is all good." Yuri smiled.

Peter and I left after supper. We went for a walk and when we returned for drinks Yuri was toasting Eric, "To the brains that regained the perimeter defense system and protected us all from the consequences of nuclear war."

Everyone joined in and then Yuri said, "Tell us how you did it Eric."

"Yuri," Eric sighed and then he continued, "It not a glorious story," Eric warned and then he shook his head and sighed again, reluctant to share, but he resigned himself and informed us, "It is one of chaos and failures in communication. It is a miracle it succeeded at all.

The planning was perfect, thanks to Captain Roberts." Eric raised his glass to Peter and then to Sayid and added, "Gaining access to the facilities at Langley was not difficult, thanks to Sayid and his men as well.

The Russians successfully gained entrance into the Moscow facility while the Chinese operatives stormed the facilities in Beijing, and the Japanese stormed Geneva in a simultaneous assault to regain the international communications system and the missile defense systems."

Eric sighed and shook his head, "Once we gained entry it was up to each of our rebel group's computer technician to access the computer system and take control of the data base. We had to do it at the same time and our watches were synchronized, but we did not allow for the slight delay in communication, nor the ability to understand one another.

We had previously agreed to communicate in English for we were all familiar with the language;

however the accents made it near impossibly to comprehend each other.

The Japanese spoke very clear English, but their technician was from Scotland. I picked him to take down Geneva, because quite frankly he was the best and Geneva was the most heavily encrypted, with a multitude of levels of security that had to be bypassed. I took Langley for the same reason.

We began to implement the plan when suddenly I was entering a series of code and I repeated the encryption back to him and it was a series of letters and numbers we all had to enter simultaneously to gain access to the entire system and they ended in, A/I_3 C 7/I T"

The Scott answered, "Aye"

The Chinese Tech said, "Are you sure this is correct?"

The Scott replied, "Of course it's correct."

"I don't think it is, 'I'. I am reading it back to you for conformation. Everybody listen carefully." The Chinese ordered. She read a long series of characters and ended, "Alpha/Indiand_3Charlie7/Indiana Tango Indiana."

"No, no" The Scott replied with irritation, "I did not mean the letter 'I'. I meant Aye as in Yes, here is the Code."

He read it out and ended it with, "...Charlie 7/Indiana Tango. Does everybody got that, it does not end in Indiana it ends in Tango. I repeat it ends with Tango"

Eric shook his head again he could not believe it and declared, "I repeated the code and ordered them to hit enter. It could have failed right then and there, but that was not our only failure in communication."

The Chinese Tech said over the com system, "Do we enter the loin?"

The Scott said, "Yes, I just told you the line of code, do you have it entered?"

"No, No, Of course I have the code entered, do I loin now?"

Eric shook his head and sighed again. I laughed slightly as he continued, "I searched my mind and said to myself, loin, loin, do I loin now? I couldn't understand the Chinese tech and then it hit me what are we supposed to do next together, oh log in, so I confirmed, "Do you mean, log in?"

"Yes that is what I said."

I gave the order to everyone, "Login in three, two, one!"

"It was a communication nightmare." Eric declared.

Peter sat back with his wine and said, "Good thing you didn't have a Spanish tech too?"

Sayid said, "Cie" and we all laughed out loud.

Eric said, "Yah well, it's funny now, but it was not so funny at the time."

"It is like a bad joke." Yuri commented, "One day there was a Scott, a China man, an American and Russian in a computer lab..."

"Yes, but it was no joke that was my day." He said somberly.

Yamamoto patted his back and smiled as he advised, "Don't worry Eric son, you should be proud; you are an honor to your country and your family. Your mission was a success; you did very well."

Yuri agreed, "Yes, now drink and be happy that it all turned out. A toast to Eric."

Everyone raised their glass and cheered, "To Eric"

Eric smiled and said, "Thank you, it was a comedy of errors in communication, but I am relieved it turned out so well."

"Still, Eric how did you stop the nuclear attack? Our plan only covered getting you access and uploading the virus." Sayid inquired.

Eric replied honestly, "I didn't; not really, I mean we entered and gained access to the enemy's communication network and we uploaded the worm as planned, I also got control of some of the satalights enabling me to activate the perimeter defense system, but it was not fully operational during the actual attack. I don't know what happened to cause the winds and tornadoes to form and bring that radiation out to sea."

Sayid looked at me as did Peter starring silently while everyone one else was distracted by Yuri's comment, "Well here's to good luck we were not all fried like chicken."

We laughed and drank together save Sayid, but we were all relishing in the calm before the storm.

Peter and I retired early as the men continued to drink and enjoy each other's company. Peter and I however only wanted to spend time alone together for in two days we would enter the Mediterranean Sea.

*****

The day of battle approached. We dressed and prepared for battle and Brother John led the troops in prayer on deck. He opened the bible and read aloud, "May the LORD answer you when you are in anguish. May the name of God... defend you. May he send you assistance from the place of safety and grant you support from Zion. May he remember all of your sacrifices and make all of your plans succeed." John closed the bible and continued his prayer for us, "May God our Creator be the strength in your arms as we fight for our freedom, may he be with you all in battle. May the Lord's holy angels go before you and may we fight with a blameless heart before our God as we await the return of our Lord"

"Amen"

As John finished his prayer a fleet of Chinese destroyers pulled up alongside us and Sayid joined us on deck and announced, "President Chang wants to meet with you, he seeks permission to board to speak with all of the rebel leaders."

Peter inquired, "How did Admiral Rodriguez respond?"

Sayid answered, "Be advised that the Admiral has the rest of the fleet moving into formation as we speak. He has said to proceed and the Captain of the ship has granted Chang and his entourage, permission to come on board, sir."

I sighed, "Very well we will meet him in the war room. Yuri, Hideki, Peter, I will join you there shortly, I need time to pray. Sayid will you join Captain Ferguson and escort Chang to the war room. John, come with me."

Everyone complied and John and I prayed together that God would fill me with wisdom and discernment and I left to join them in the war room.

Everyone was sitting around a large table and stood as I arrived. Captain Ferguson pulled out his chair for me and said, "Here you go Commander, I will leave you all to your meeting."

Before the Captain departed he warned, "President Chang we are entering hostile waters in two hours. I suggest you make your way safely to your ship before our arrival. Good day."

The Captain of the ship left us and all was silent for a while I assessed Chang and his men. He was not alone, but aside from his own security three other high ranking party officials joined him and stood behind Chang. Their security details waited outside with Marines watching over them

I calmly inquired, "So President Chang, why are you here and why is a fleet of your destroyers on our doorstep?"

President Chang answered, "China has decided to join you in your battle against the dictator Augustus and his forces, while you are freeing Jerusalem, we will ensure your victory on the seas."

Peter stares coldly at Chang as he states, "The British navy is already en-route to join us, as is half of Russian fleet. Why would you join us after orchestrating a nuclear attack that could have annihilated all of us and why on earth would we trust you?"

Chang answers were void of emotion, "We did attempt to destroy both the New World Order and nations who support religious extremes in a coordinated effort to bring about a new era of peace. We failed and we were mistaken in perpetuating that attack, but the people of China have demanded that we support you and your allies in defeating Augustus and Lumen.

Your public announcement has led to revolutionary unrest in China Commander Miles." I was relieved that he did not know I was now Catherine Roberts, but I did not show my emotions as he continued, "In order to keep the peace we have decided to secure a peace and an alliance with you."

I informed him, "I have no problem with the people of China President Chang, but I do have a problem with you. I do not trust you or your government. If you publicly announce right now that you will step down as leader, I will take it a sign of good faith on your part and accept a temporary alliance with China."

He replied grudgingly, "You ask much, the people of China would be pleased if the alliance is secured and Augustus defeated, but I cannot give in to such a demand."

I responded without hesitation, "Then there is no alliance and nothing to discuss."

A party official whispered something in the president's ear. He then replied, "Very well, I agree to your terms."

I turned to Sayid and ordered, "Sayid please call for Eric to set up a video feed and prepare for a broadcast to China."

"Now?" President Chang was shocked.

"Now!" I replied firmly.

Hideki declared, "The people of China will be pleased to see how seriously you are taking their wishes to heart and comforted by our presence, a sure sign of our impending alliance and future relationship."

Eric was with Sayid as he reported, "Everything is ready commander."

"You're on President Chang, just look up at the screen across from you. When the light turns green you may make your announcement." Eric informed him.

Chang replied, "I am willing to cooperate, but this is foolish, you are warning Augustus that we are united and preparing an attack."

"It is a secure link to China and no other transmissions will be allowed to leave China following the message." Eric assured him.

"It is impossible to control that." Chang responded.

"Difficult, but not impossible." Eric smirked.

"Now prepare to address your nation." I ordered.

Chang sat up tall and began his speech, "Today I would like to announce to the People's Republic of China, that I President Chang, have secured an Alliance with Catherine Miles and her fellow leaders in the Resistance. We will support the Resistance and their allies against the dictator Augustus and his false god Lumen.

As a sign of this alliance and our commitment to them I would first like to apologize for the nuclear attack that was launched against them under my watch. I would like to inform the allies and the world that this attack was not supported or sanctioned by the Chinese people and I am formally announcing my resignation as president today.

It is my fervent hope that this alliance will grow into a long-term relationship of peace. It was my pleasure serving the people of China and I leave you in good hands."

I then assured the people as Eric's software translated my words for the Chinese people without changing my voice, "I would like to thank the people of China for their bravery and courage in holding their government to account through your recent mass demonstrations. We know and understand how difficult it was to stand against your own government at a time such as this. I am confident that your nation will rise to honor and become a faithful ally in the future.

Today I can promise you that we in the resistance do not hold the people of China personally responsible for the horrible actions of your former ruler. We in the resistance do not condone any form of vengeance, or retaliation for this strike and we accept your alliance in destroying the dictator Augustus. We wish you all peace, prosperity and freedom. This is Commander Catherine Miles, speaking on behalf of the resistance. Thank you for your support."

The transmission ended and I turned to face Chang, "Tell your fleet they are welcome to join us and that we welcome their cooperation and support and then inform them that you will be remaining onboard as our guest. We have many things to discuss Chang."

Chang then passed on the information to the fleet, which also herd the announcement, so his mandatory stay was not challenged, especially by the higher party officials, who were pleased to have Chang step down and open the era to new leadership.

Politics is a dirty backstabbing business and the officials looked pleased by Chang's detention with us. I am sure it protected them from retaliation from Chang's supporters within the regime and party itself. Chang did not look so pleased, as his officials left without a word.

Hideki asked, "Chang, I like Commander Miles do not trust you, but I do believe you want to destroy Augustus and Lumen, however how do we know

China will not turn that massive fleet on us once the enemies' fleet is destroyed?"

Chang responded, "You don't, but how many Russian vessels can you be sure are loyal to you in this attack. The Russian government coordinated with me in the nuclear strike; China was not alone in this."

Yuri scoffs, "The Russian government yes, politicians like you Chang, but I can assure you every captain and ranking officer on those Russian vessels are loyal to me and Mother Russia, not to our corrupted government officials, who sacrifice everything to grasp for power."

Peter agreed, "Chang you politicians underestimate the fighting men and women who serve in all levels of the armed forces. We are not loyal to a particular politician, to a ruler or government; we are loyal to our nations, our people and our ideals. You politicians foolishly mistake that allegiance as something owed to you personally; it is only given to the leaders who are serving their nations not their own personal interests. I promise you every vessel in our fleet is dedicated to our cause."

"You answer to your, Commander in Chief, President Davidson, Captain. The military is not an independent force. Even if the rebels are independent, the military in all of your countries still answers to the political elite." Chang countered.

Hideki then said, "That was before Lumen's rise to power and Augustus' dictatorship Chang, and you know it. Nothing is as it was before."

Peter stated, "So we are very sure as to our ships, however trusting your fleet is another serious issue. We must have some way of ensuring that your fleet does not have orders to attack us once Augustus is destroyed. Perhaps, if you gave us the launch codes and access to your systems we could feel more comfortable with this alliance."

Chang was offended and protested, "I cannot give you such sensitive information! It is too much that you ask. Would any of you give me yours? No, I don't think so, besides as soon as I stepped down as leader they would have changed the access codes and removed my ability to access any system."

Peter realized we were at a stalemate, so he ordered Sayid, "Bring the Captain back here. Eric, connect with the Admiral."

Sayid returned shortly with the ship's Captain and Admiral Rodriguez spoke to us on screen. "Captain Ferguson, Admiral Rodriguez, the Chinese have generously offered to support us in the attack that is now less than two hours away and considering their recent acts of aggression, there is concern that they may turn on us after they have completed the assault on Augustus fleet. I suggest that we have the Chinese vessels head the assault with an ally's destroyer on either side of them and at their stern. We will attack in formation for as long as possible. The British and the Canadian fleet will take up the rear and escort them back out to sea after the battle."

Yuri spoke, "They have far more submarines than us and this could pose an even greater risk."

Peter turned to Eric, "Eric can you hack in and track the movements of the entire fleet, especially the Chinese?"

Eric pondered it and then replied, "I could if I was fluent in Chinese, but I'm not familiar with Asian characters and I don't have time to alter the programming for the translation software. The lag in translation would result in immediate failure."

Chang's former personal body guard and Hideki's nephew Akiro Daiki spoke up, "I am fluent in all Asian languages and I was a low level computer administrator when Chang hired me. Once he discovered who I was he hired me to be his personal bodyguard. I fear my computer skills are seriously lacking compared to Eric's though."

Eric smiled as he assured Akiro, "No problem I can walk you through it. Permission to leave, we need to begin preparations immediately."

Admiral Rodriguez replied, "Permission granted."

Then the Admiral ordered, "Captain Ferguson, have Chang escorted to secure quarters."

Yuri added, "And have him searched for any tools of espionage."

Chang said, "I assure you Commander, I am not betraying you, we cannot defeat Augustus unless we as world leaders are united against him. My political counterparts, have been unwilling, except for Bourbon, to publicly take a formal stance against the New World Order. I have from the beginning."

I pondered this for a moment and Hideki replied, "Yes you have Chang, you have been bold and outspoken against Augustus and Lumen, but China had the luxury of being the most powerful nation on earth. You could afford to be insolent."

Yuri then added, "Furthermore you publicly denounced an American alliance as well. You wanted China to stand alone at the top and bring about a new empire and failed. You tried to annihilate anyone you perceived as a threat. Your alliance is tactical, and merely political maneuvering, but the Chinese people want more."

The Admiral declared , "We all do, so we will capitalize on this opportunity to defeat the New World Order and free Jerusalem, but you will never gain my trust Chang or the trust of the American People. We simply acknowledge that the New World Order cannot be defeated unless we unite, as temporary and fleeting as that union may be."

Yuri then added, "Chang you better not betray us, for if you do, I will be the first to bring you much pain and suffering."

Captain Ferguson ordered the MP's, "Take our guest to his quarters, search him and send forth a report to the bridge and for now he is confined to quarters."

The MP replied, "Aye, aye Captain."

Gentlemen, you better report to your ships, good luck. Admiral, permission to return to the bridge and prepare to disembark."

"Permission granted and God bless you all. Admiral Rodriguez signing off."

I expressed my gratitude, "Thank you for your time gentlemen. I will see you in Jerusalem."

They all left and Chang was taken into custody. After everyone cleared the room, Peter walked toward me and stated, "We were in the eye of the storm, the calm has come to an end and the battle begins, but no matter what becomes of us. I am thankful we go to war together. I love you"

I smiled as I replied, "Me too, I will love you forever and always."

Peter kissed me, "Let's head to the roof to see Yuri and the commanders off."

I laughed, "The roof? A ship has a roof?"

Peter smiled informed me, "It is navy speak for the flight deck."

He kissed me again and then we walked out to the flight deck.

Peter and I would enter battle joined forever as one. We remained on deck after the other commanders returned to their ships as we looked out at the enemy fleet before us. Our massive fleet moved forward in formation as the sirens roared and everyone ready to face what lay before them.

*****

Chapter Eight: In Enemy Hands.

Peter and I went to our quarters and prepared to leave the ship. He had his dagger guns holstered and Jacob handed him the sword he was given in the Rockies. Peter had it strapped to his back in a specialized sheath and carried a light machine gun as well. I took along four of the throwing knives that Yamomoto gave me, as did Peter. Before we entered the Mediterranean Sea the British and French Naval forces announced their arrival.

I urged, "Peter stay by my side throughout the battle." He nodded and kissed me quickly one last time before the bloodshed began.

The unmanned drones were launched first setting off the surface the air missiles of the enemy's perimeter defense systems and a squadron set out to knock out some of the enemy's radar systems preventing the launch of further surface to air missiles.

Then more fighter jets had taken off before we entered enemy waters, but a few that could have vertical take offs remained with some choppers.

We got on helicopters and as others boarded the remaining fighters. We were headed for Jerusalem itself with ammunition and medical supplies. Peter, Eric, John, Sky and Jacob flew with me on the chopper and Sayid was our pilot.

The Israelis were expecting us, but so where enemy forces. The heavy artillery and missiles that were previously targeting Israel were focused on the sea of warships that lay before them. A few small surface- to- air missiles targeted our aircraft, but they did not succeed in taking us out.

I heard Hideki declare over the communications system, "Clear the path gentlemen."

I looked out my window as the Japanese fighter jets flew past us suddenly, surging ahead firing their heat seeking missiles.

I recognized Soku's voice warning, "Watch your six Firefly."

Sayid had a special helmet that gave him a three hundred and sixty view of the battle field and some of our allies wore the same helmets.

Our ally fighters flew ahead past us into enemy territory. The American jets flew higher above us. The Raptors and the Veloci-Raptors had stealth technology making them invisible to any radar. They soared and could dive down instantaneously flying at well over 2200 miles per hour, they did not have to use after-burn to achieve top speeds that far exceeded the speed of light and easily broke the sound barrier and sustained flight, six times the speed of sound for extended periods of time.

The enemy had stealth technology too, but their technology was older making their stealth planes weaker, slower and fewer in numbers.

The American fighter jets were far more advanced than any other fighter jet in the world. The New World Order managed to get control of a squad of F22 Raptors, but President Davidson managed to secretly produce and guard the next advanced generation; the Veloci-Raptors, which were even faster and better armed, and more maneuverable than their predecessor, able to fly outside the earth's atmosphere and re-enter from outer space.

They had taken out all of the satalights that Eric did not have access too. The enemy could not track us on land or sea anymore and their communication systems crippled but the demonic realm still relayed information swiftly and effectively.

We flew low and even though the chopper was advanced, it could still be detected by the enemy below us and we were thankful for our allies flying ahead, behind and far above us undetected by the enemy.

Our new Veloci-Raptor could not be detected by the enemy. They could track and identify most of the ally planes, and we could detect theirs too, with exception to the few F22's which surely would share their skies.

Peter had Eric hack into all of Davidson files and all military developments in America. We kept very close tabs on the North American President. Intel was essential to the survival and empowerment of the militia and I was indebted to Eric and Peter for our success. Thankfully the words, Top Secret and Classified, did not apply to the greatest hacker in the world. Thank God for Eric, he truly was a gift from God.

John looked worried, so I touched his knee and reassured him, "Don't worry, you had a dream. You get to Jerusalem, remember."

John grinned and declared, I'm not worried about, me. I know that I'll be there. It is everyone else I am concerned about, especially you."

I loved that he still worried about me, but I assured him, "Don't fret John; I know my destiny. I can protect myself, and I am in very good hands."

John held my hand and declared, "You are; forgive me. We'll be fine."

Kato was heard saying, "Fire Fox, Bogie at three o'clock."

Soku replied, "I'm on it, Fire Fly watch it, two more flying toward you at nine and eleven."

Akiro warned, "Black hawk red hot fireworks six o'clock."

Sayid released heat seeking flares that drew a missile away from us.

Hideki then announced, "Entering Israeli air space. Israeli flock approaches."

"Roger that returning in twenty gentlemen. Thank you Fire Fly I have entered Israeli Airspace." Sayid informed them.

"Welcome Black Hawk we will lead you in, you are cleared for landing." An Israeli fighter declared.

The ariel ballet of the fighter jets would continue in the skies above while the Sea battle in the Mediterranean would go on in our absence. We had another mission. We had to reach Jerusalem with desperately needed supplies and military equipment. The armies of the world continued to engage each other in battle as we landed on Israeli soil.

We landed outside Tel Aviv, two more choppers landed behind us loaded with medical supplies.

Sayid announced, "I have another run to do Commander; I will meet you in Jerusalem."

I replied, "Fly safe, I'll see you soon."

We watched Sayid fly off as we waited for the Israeli transport. As we watched Sayid flying back toward the sea a black F22 suddenly dropped from the sky descending on him like an angel of death from above.

Another F22 fell into position right behind him. Just as we feared we would witness Sayid's certain death, three Veloci- Raptors flew in formation taking out the two enemy Raptors with ease. We cheered elated that Sayid was saved.

Instantaneously a few Russian SU 47's dropped low and engaged the Veloci-Raptors in a dog fight. The Russian's fired their heat seeking missiles on the American jests.

John said, "I thought the Russians were on our side?"

"The rebels are and most of the Russian fleet, but the Russian government sided with Augustus and Lumen." Peter replied.

The heat seeking missiles could not lock onto the Veloci-Raptors and John looked puzzled, so Peter informed him, "The Veloci-Raptors fly by cold infusion technology that ensures that next to no heat signature is present, but if necessary it can fly across the globe through space at super-sonic speeds. Don't worry John nothing can outfly her."

Moments later a missile from the waters below targeted Sayid's chopper. We saw Sayid's helicopter blown from the sky. "God no!" I yelled and then we saw a parachute open in the skies above. Sayid was safe for now, but he would be falling in hostile waters.

"Don't worry Catherine he's a Seal, he is prepared for a situation like this, I guarantee it." Peter comforted me. "I'll order a chopper to fly in and pick him up."

An Israeli transport picked us up with most of the supplies and drove us toward Jerusalem intending to drive through a series of underground tunnels.

Before we neared the tunnel, Peter ordered Eric, "Open your laptop, can you get a satellite read on Sayid."

Eric obeyed immediately, "Our satellite will be in position any minute...Yes sir. He's alive. He is moving slowly in the water toward land."

"Order one of our choppers to go and pick him up." I commanded

"We can't Commander; he is right between the Israeli ships and the Syrians. We will have to wait till our battleships reach further inland and defeat Augusts' forces at sea. Sayid will make contact as soon as he reaches safety." Eric declared confidently.

"Not if the enemy reaches him first." I replied.
John said, "We will pray they don't."

I did not join John in his prayer as he bowed his head I announced, "Eric I'm going to get Sayid, you keep me posted." I banged on the truck and it came to a halt. I jumped out and then I ordered, "Continue on to Jerusalem with John and Sky. Captain Roberts, Jacob and I are going back for Sergeant Sayid."

Peter banged on the truck and ordered the Israeli transport driver "Move out."

The Israeli officer said "I will call for another vehicle, Captain." We had not driven far so it was not long before a driver picked us up headed for the coast.

Peter relayed, "Eric notified me that Sayid has made contact. He is onboard a Syrian vessel, the Zada"

"How did he get onboard, is he okay?" I inquired.

"Negative, he has activated his tracking beacon on his watch. He may be captured, but they have not discovered it yet." Peter answered, listening carefully to Eric through his RF device.

Eric had designed special watches for our entire unit, to track us should any of us fall into enemy hands.

I was thankful and praised God and prayed to myself, "God bless Eric and protect Sayid."

I turned to the Israeli officer and said, "We need a helicopter immediately."

The officer warned, "Commander, it's a suicide mission, if you're not blown from the sky en-route you would be tortured and killed as soon as you board the ship."

"I'll take my chances, now get me a chopper" I ordered.

"Commander he's right. We will surely be killed, we will rescue Sergeant Sayid, but we must do so with stealth and planning, if we are to succeed." Peter advised.

"He does not have long Captain; I will not have him tortured and killed. I will not leave him in enemy hands." I declared.

Peter whispered in my ear so that the Israeli soldier with us did not hear him speaking to me in a familiar way.

"Catherine, trust me my love. Give me time to come up with a feasible plan." Peter pleaded

I informed him, "You have one hour to come up with a plan and then I am going in."

"One hour, give me two at least." Peter said sarcastically.

Peter looked to the Israeli soldier, "Do you have any Syrian sailors in custody who have sailed on the Zada?"

"I will find out sir." the soldier replied.

Peter contacted Eric, "Lieutenant, we need to know everything we can about that ship."

Eric replied, "I'm already working on it sir, according to our naval intelligence it is the, Moscow. It is an old, Russian class destroyer sold to the Syrians a decade ago. She flies under both the old Syrian flag and New World Older above that. She is the only Syrian ship left in Augustus' fleet."

Peter told Eric, "Contact Commander Michaelovich and see if he or his men know anything about that particular vessel, relay to us any pertinent information."

"Roger that." Eric replied
Eric continued and informed us, "I already know that Commander Michaelovich and his men served on the Moscow over a decade ago. He and his men are ex-navy, Captain. I'll contact him ASAP."

The Israeli soldier notified us, "My commander is on her way. She should be here in five minutes, and we do have a Syrian sailor in custody and a Syrian operative on board."

"What operative?" Peter inquired.

He answered, "The sailor's mate serves on that ship too. She is the communications officer. We have promised to keep her husband alive and unharmed if she feeds us pertinent information."

"Hmm, does she believe in the self-proclaimed god: is she loyal to Augustus?" I asked.

"No, few Syrians are, they simply hate us Jews. They are playing to Augustus and his god to gain an upper hand in the war. Decades of civil war followed by attacks on Israel have left them in a state of desperation. Prior to the rise of the dictator and following their civil war, Syria was losing to us badly." He explained. "We have dominated the

Mediterranean Sea and destroyed much of their fleet prior to the dictator's rise to power."

Eric informed us and Peter relayed, "Commander Michaelovich and his men are making their way towards us as we speak."

As we waited for Yuri and his men to arrive the Israeli commander moved toward us. "Commander Miles, Captain Roberts, I am pleased to meet you. I am Commander Amiti."

"Hello commander, this is Jacob." I replied.

The commander bowed her head slightly and then she said, "You may call me Shoshanna."

I responded, "Pleased to meet you Shoshanna, you may call me Catherine."

"One of my men is aboard the Zada. We are awaiting our Russian comrades and then we will rescue him. We would like to speak to your Syrian prisoner as well. We would appreciate any Intel you could provide." I declared.

"I cannot sacrifice any men in your rescue mission, however we will cooperate with you in any way we can." She assured me.

Just as she declared this Yuri and his men approached with the Japanese Hercules fighter jets falling in behind. The commander looked surprised to see the Russians and the Japanese approach and come awaiting my command.

"Sergeant Sayid has been captured by the enemy; I will not give them time to torture and kill him. Every minute that passes only prolongs his agony. Commander Michaelovich will you ride with us and tell us everything you know about that ship. Thank you for coming, Commander Yamomoto. We are indebted to you and your men." I bowed slightly after saying this.

He nodded and I said, "Commander Yuri Michaelovich, Commander Yamomoto this is Commander Amiti."

Yuri said, "Ah, Israeli intelligence, I have heard of you commander."

Yamomoto said nothing he just bowed his head slightly.

Commander Amiti replied, "Hello Commander Michaelovich, I hear you once commanded aboard the vessel you Russians sold to the Syrians."

"Yes I did, she is a beautiful and powerful vessel, but not without her failings. Mother Russia has long profited from selling weapons and various vessels to your enemies. It is a very ugly face of war and of our history, not our finest hour." Yuri shrugged

"No, it wasn't, but no matter, we have destroyed much of our enemy's ships and we have stayed ahead of them in technology, praise be to God." Amiti added.

A second larger transport arrived and we were all about to climb in and share Intel so that we could formulate a plan and then Shoshanna said, "Captain you may ride with me if you wish."

Inadvertently I clenched my fist and felt a possessive rage rise up with in me, but Peter declined, "Thank you commander, but I must ride with Commander Michaelovich and debrief."

"As you wish Captain." She replied and moved toward her jeep with her officer at her side. She obviously was unaware of any of our relationships to one another and unnerved by our association with the Russians. I could not let anyone know that Peter and I were together, it could place him at risk.

Yamomoto cautioned, "My dear Catherine you must hide your affections for the Captain while on this mission. It is a weakness that enemies will capitalize on, if they have a chance."

"Hideki is correct, I thought you would have slit her pretty throat and she is on our side." Yuri chuckled, "Good thing her eyes were on Roberts and she paid little attention to you."

Peter added, "They're both right. This Syrian and his lover are both compromised and they are being used and manipulated by their enemies because of their relationship to one another. We must both be careful and hide our feelings for each other; no one here must know that we are husband and wife."

I nodded in agreement and said, "You all are wise in your counsel, but you will have to firmly keep Shoshanna at bay, because I do believe that if she places one hand on you in a familiar way, I may break her arm."

They laughed at me and Peter smiled and then he answered, "Yes dear." Then he focused on Yuri and said, "So Yuri, tell us everything we need to know about that ship."

Yuri pulled out his tablet projector and gave us a detailed account of the layout and then where the brig was, "This is where they are likely to hold Sayid. There is an access hatch two floors above it near the stairs at the bow of the ship."

Peter studied the schematics and then asked, "What is the best way to get onboard that ship without being noticed?"

Yuri smiled and said, "Well, there is a glitch in the radar system during storms and rough seas. It cannot pick up other vessels and objects in the water nearby. It fails to get accurate readings." Then Yuri sighed, "Too bad we cannot control the weather, so I am afraid we cannot get onboard going undetected."

"You will have your storm Yuri." I assured him.

He raised an eyebrow and then continued as he shrugged his broad shoulders, "Well the access hatch will be locked in the event of a storm, so we must climb on board the ship from the sea below, not an easy task in stormy seas."

We planned on borrowing some personal submersibles and approach the ship during the height of the storm, and then we would climb up the side of the ship and make our way toward the brig. We hoped to rescue Sayid and leave before anyone knew we were there. We would have to kill anyone we encountered by hand. We agreed that we should not utilize any fire arms that could only result in raising further awareness our presence, except for Yuri and Peter who had their silencers with them.

We arrived at the Israeli detention center and Jacob held his hand out toward us, "I'll hold your wedding rings."

Commander Amiti joined us and led us to her prisoner. Yuri offered to question the prisoner and we watched from a room next store, Peter went in with Yuri as well.

Yuri said, "We are going to make this short and sweet, we would like you to quickly tell us the times and schedules of guards on watch tonight aboard the Moscow."

The Syrian prisoner replied, "I do not have detailed knowledge of such things."

Peter suggested, "Then why don't you tell us what you do know?"

The Syrian said cockily, "Why should I tell you anything? My agreement is with the Israelis, not you."

Peter said, "Jacob, Vladimir could you please come in here?"

Jacob looked at me and I nodded confirmation and Hideki and Akiro stepped forward and stood on either side of me, so Jacob and Vladimir left us.

As the large Russian warrior and Jacob entered the room as Yuri replied, "Because boy, we are not Israeli, and you are correct, we have no agreement with you. We will have your cooperation one way, or another."

The Syrian swallowed as both Jacob and Vladimir towered above him, showing no emotion as they stared down at him. The Syrian cooperated telling us, "There are a total of six guards walking the upper deck and two guards on duty outside the brig. Two more men with machine guns are on the towers at the bow and the stern.

Syrians man the guns, but it is Augustus' forces that walk on guard duty. They switch every six hours at six, and twelve. They are never late for shift change. You cannot defeat these men, but these two may."

"Thank you for your cooperation." Yuri said as they turned to leave.

The Syrian inquired, "What are you planning, is Kythira in danger?"

"No, she's safe." Peter assured him and then they left the prisoner, who looked relieved.

Commander Amiti said, "Captain Roberts is impressive."

I clenched my teeth and made no reply as Hideki gently squeezed my arm and he declared, "Yes he is a remarkable, leader and the epitome of self-control."

Shoshanna frowned as she asked, "What do you mean."

Hideki answered, "He never loses focus; he is completely dedicated to the mission, his men and his commanders. He never allows anything, or anyone to distract him. Indeed he is impressive that way; I am honored to say he was my student for a time."

I was thankful for Hideki's diplomatic intercession. My thoughts returned to Sayid. I feared that Sayid was already being tortured, but I knew he loved Mary and now she was expecting their first child, he would do everything to survive. Still, we had to get him back. We had to save him for her. As I thought of Sayid, Yuri and Peter walked in.

Yuri said, "Well that was easy."

Peter added, "Yes, but the coward offered information to save himself, possibly placing his lover at risk."

Shoshanna countered, "I don't know, I saw love in his eyes when he inquired as to your plans."

Yamomoto interjected, "Yes it appeared so, but he loved himself more, he cooperated out of fear, self-preservation, or..." Yamomoto pondered.

Peter nodded and finished his sentence, "...or he gave us faulty information, hoping we would fail and not succeed in our mission, thereby protecting Kythira."

"There is no guessing what his motivations are, we will not rely on the Intel. Is there a way to contact Kythira and ask her the same questions? Then we can compare their answers." I sated.

Commander Amiti responded, "I will have Intel make contact with Kythira immediately."

"Thank you Commander." I responded and then continued, "We will wait for confirmation then move out, however if we do not here by 21:00 hours we will move out regardless, agreed?

"Agreed." They all replied in unison.

I thanked Shoshanna as I said, "Thank you Commander Amiti, for granting us access to your prisoner. May we borrow some personal submersibles?"

"Of course, but first, if you would like to come with me we have supper waiting for you. Our president is excited about dining with you Commander." She replied without hesitation.

"I apologize, but I don't have time. I have other things I must attend to." I informed her. I was annoyed that she would even expect my attendance at such a time as this.

Hideki smiled and said, "We made our plan to board the vessel tonight and launch a rescue mission under the cover of darkness and the coming storm. We have time for dinner. There is little else we can do this evening."

Yuri supported Hideki saying, "I agree the plan is set, we should eat."

The Israeli commander looked pleased and replied, "The President will be delighted; I will inform him at once, but I can assure you the weather will be clear tonight. There is nothing on the radar, we keep meticulous track of the weather."

"Gentlemen enjoy you meal, but I really must decline. I have something which must be done." I declared.

I turned to leave and Peter and Jacob followed me. Shoshanna was disturbed and coaxed, "Commander, I understand that whatever you feel you must do takes precedence over dinner, however surely you could spare your men. They must eat."

Hideki interjected before I had time to answer and he said, "Commander Amiti, I am sure you understand our paranoia. We as Commanders in the

Resistance never go anywhere without our personal guards, Commander Miles especially. Her men are bound to stay by her side. I know you and the president understand this."

Shoshanna relented, "Of course, forgive me. Follow me gentlemen. I will show you the way out and then I will escort you to dinner, while Commander Miles attends to her business"

We needed to launch a rescue mission under the cover of darkness and the storm, which I would pray forth. I had not heard from God for a long time now, but I trusted that he still heard me.

Peter spoke as we approached a place by the water. He inquired, "So my love, what is it we are doing here?"

I answered honestly, "You and Jacob can stand guard. Don't let anyone, or anything near me. This may take hours. When I pray forth something this big, there are moments that I am not aware of anything else around me. It is what some refer to as willing, but I know it is the power of prayer. I will pray forth a storm. If you are uncomfortable with this, Jacob is enough to protect me."

Peter looked skeptical, but he said, "No love, I think this is one of those things that I need to see to believe."

"You already saw it in the mountains and it freaked you out a little." I teased.

Peter laughed, "Well sudden wind in the mountains is not an uncommon thing."

"Yes my dear Captain, nor is it uncommon at sea either. What will it take to convince you my love?"

Peter shrugged his shoulders and I kissed his cheek and then sat and began to pray.

It took a few hours, so Peter went over the plan in his head. He recalled every detail of the mission, while I sat cross legged facing the ocean praying.

I was not filled with the ancient Aramaic words this time, but I did focus my mind, my heart and my faith as I raised my hands I declared aloud, "Oh Lord my God you are sovereign over all of creation, Jesus you said in your word that what I believe will be, what I ask I will receive. You said that, we would do greater things than you and you clamed the seas, I ask that you use me and raise them. Raise them, raise them now." I lifted my hands toward the waters and I called forth the clouds to congregate above the enemy ships, I called forth the winds to toss the seas and disrupt the ocean, I ordered the earth below the ocean floor to rumble.

The storm began to rise and the storm grew in strength and power as Shoshanna cleared her throat behind Peter. Peter placed his finger to his lips and she watched silently as Jacob and Peter stood guard.

I did not know she was watching me. When I finished and the storm had reached its zenith. I got up and faced her as she said in amazement, "How is it that you speak ancient Hebrew?"

"I do not, Yeshua simply allowed you to hear what you needed to. " Yeshua was the Hebrew name for Jesus and I smiled, "The spirit of God spoke forth through me."

"It is true, the rumors about you, you have the adoration of men, the ear of God, and do you have the strength of his arm as well?" She inquired unnerved by what she witnessed.

I looked to Jacob and then I answered honestly, "I do, but so do all who believe in him. He gives each according to their faith, but even my faith was given from above. I did not develop it, I did not earn it. He gave that to me as well."

She stared at me a little mesmerized and suspicious and I continued, "You have something for me?"

"Yes I do commander, the submersibles are ready and your team is assembled and prepared to depart." She stood at attention.

I said, "Thank you commander; lead the way."

Peter inquired as we departed, "What was it you heard, Commander Amiti?"

She turned and answered plainly, " Jesus call to the winds and make the storm come forth."

"I heard the same thing." Peter responded.

"Yes, but I heard it in the Hebrew tongue, you heard it in English didn't you?" Amiti questioned further, "How is this possible?"

Peter replied, "I don't know, but the Christian bible refers it to…"

Commander Amiti interjected, "speaking in tongues. If this is true, what does this mean? What is the significance?"

"Trust me Commander, you are asking the wrong person that question." Peter informed her.

Commander Amiti looked surprised and inquired, "You are not a believer then, Captain? I am surprised; you seem so... loyal to her."

Peter smiled as he looked back over his shoulder to me and then answered, "Commander Miles does not demand that her men believe what she believes and our loyalty is not based upon a single faith, but rather a single purpose."

"So you are not loyal to Catherine alone?" Shoshanna asked in a hushed tone, unaware that I could still hear her conversation with Peter even though I was a few paces behind them with Jacob at my side.

Peter spoke in a calm cold tone as he assured her, "Commander Amiti, I am completely loyal to Commander Miles as a person, we all are. We would sacrifice our lives for her without hesitation and there is almost nothing we wouldn't do for her. She commands and we obey. I just don't share her belief structure, but don't take that to mean that I am not loyal to her."

Commander Amiti replied, "That's good Captain, we should be loyal to our superiors, I did not intend any offence to your honor."

Peter responded without emotion, "None taken Commander."

She glanced at his ring finger and inquired, "Are you married Captain?"

"Why do you ask?" Peter retorted.

Amiti took hold of his hand and I clenched my fist as she said, "I was wondering because I noticed that you have a tan line where a ring was recently worn."

Peter laughed, "I was married not so long ago."

"What happened?" She inquired batting her eyes at him tilting her head slightly.

Peter took his hand away and rubbed his hands saying, "Well I married a crazy, jealous woman. I must say she's nuts. A woman would just look at me or touch me in any familiar way and she would break her arm. It kind of scared me off all other women. I'll never be walking down the aisle with another woman again."

I ginned and shook my head as we walked behind them and I placed two leather gloves on my hands to hide my ring hand as Shoshanna laughed, "Well Captain we are not all that extreme, but a part of me understands. If you were my man, I wouldn't want another woman touching you either. Perhaps you will consider giving another woman a chance, go out with me next time you're in Telaviv." She finished speaking as she rubbed Peter's soldier.

"Well I'm flattered, really Commander, but I can't shake this feeling, like I could die any moment now." Peter stated.

Shoshanna smiled, "All the more reason to embrace every moment, Captain."

We arrived and everyone was ready to depart. I barked, "Prepare to depart immediately gentlemen."

Peter and the men obeyed.

Jacob felt my rage and spoke for me. "Thank you for your assistance Commander Amiti."

"God's speed, I look forward to your safe return." Amiti replied

Yuri observed how Amiti looked directly at the Captain and when she left he laughed. "Oh Peter you are in deep water now."

"You have no idea Yuri, please let it go." Peter pleaded

'Da, I can see this storm has nothing on your wife's tempest." He chuckles.

I boarded my submersible and set off.

"Move out." Hideki ordered.

So we made our way through the rough waters toward the enemy ship. Lighting ripped across the sky above us and the dark waters roared in reply. Our personal submersibles scooted through the ocean and we anchored them below the enemy ship. We used suction cups as we made our way up the side of the ship near the bow. Peter whispered, "I'm glad we trained climbing that mountain face for all those months. That was hard work."

I smiled to myself and did not comment, still I thought, 'God works all things for good, he prepared us each for this mission.' I knew we would succeed in saving Sayid.

We got onboard and below deck undetected. We hid in the shadows and made our way down the stairs unnoticed and then Jacob and Vladimir took out the guards outside the door where we thought they were holding Sayid.

Peter and I entered the room and Sayid was in the process of being tortured. We surprised the interrogator who said, "How dare you disturb my session?" He turned and said, "What is the reason…"

Vladimir elbowed the interrogator in the nose with as Peter disarmed the Syrian torturer with ease. Yuri fell in behind us and removed Sayid's restraints. I knelt before him and placed my hand on his knee and I asked, "Sayid are you all right? Can you walk?"

Sayid nodded, "The torturer just arrived, and the interrogation hasn't been long. I'm only a little roughed up."

Sayid got up and continued, "I know that they have nuclear missiles. I saw them before I was captured. They were planning a launch before the storm arose and delayed the attack. They plan on launching at dawn. We cannot allow Israel to fall, they will annihilate her." Sayid warned.

I looked toward Yuri, "Okay Yuri, where do we go?"

"This way, we need to split up. Two must disable the launch computers and the rest will go and disarm the missiles themselves, but both are heavily guarded. The computer systems are Syrian and Augusts may have reprogrammed them too, but…" Yuri grinned and continued, "…there is a hidden subroutine in every Russian vessel. We did it so that the vessels and weapons that we sold could never be used against us."

"Genius! You Russians are a shrewd bunch." Hideki remarked.

"Yes this is true, we must all protect mother Russia." Yuri winked.

"Okay, Yuri take your men, Vladimir, Andrei and Michael and disable those computers, Catherine, Jacob, Sayid and I will make our way with Hideki, Akiro, Kato and Soku to the missiles and we will disable the nukes." Peter ordered.

Everybody nodded and began our new mission. Sayid led us to the missals below deck. We were faced with taking out two armed soldiers outside the door. Jacob took one and Soku and I faced off against the other. He was so fearsome and strong that he literally laughed at my attempts to harm him. We engaged in hand to hand combat in a narrow corridor after both of us had been thrown into the steel doors behind us, Hideki and Kato and Peter attacked as well. The space was limited and Hideki and Kato were exceptionally effective with their short and swift punches, but they too were thrown and kicked down the hall. Akiro held his own with a swiftness and agility few could match.

Jacob surprisingly still had his hands full as the two giants pushed each other back and forth against the wall. It was getting louder than we expected so Hideki, Kato, Peter and I all pulled our knives and daggers simultaneously and attacked our targets.

Hideki slid low and sliced the first soldier that we were fighting in the back tendon of his knees. As he collapsed Kato swiftly slid a blade across his throat.

Peter tuned toward Jacob's foe. He held Jacob by the throat and was about to stab him with a dagger. Peter pulled out his gun and shot the villain in the head. Jacob stepped back and nodded his thanks, as we witnessed red mist escape from the body of the deceased. Green mist slithered from the bodies of the other bodies

"What the Hell is that?" Peter uttered.

Jacob caught his breath as he said, "Demons."

Hideki nodded, "We have heard of such fearsome warriors in our legends of old, they will wonder the ship and inhabit another. Their dark magic is strong and they prefer the body of a warrior; we called it, Saigo no Nindou, the Spirit of the Ninja, but they will inhabit any empty vessel to survive, man or beast. We must hurry."

We opened the doors and the missile room was empty save a few Syrian technicians. They saw the bodies of Augustus' Special Forces lying dead outside, so they did not resist us, they stepped back in fear, but one of them drew his gun and said, "Stay back, or I'll shoot."

Peter had his gun aimed at the Syrian while I replied, "Lower your weapon and we will let you live." We could all see that he was afraid.

The Syrian threatened, "I will kill you, stay back."

In an instant Jacob was at his side, with his arm behind his back and Soku was not far behind as he had a blade held to his throat as he said, "You can't kill her, she has already died. Are you ready to die?"

The Syrian swallowed and then pleaded for his life, "No, please have mercy. Don't kill me."

Soku turned and looked at me and I ordered, "Let him go Soku, Jacob release him. He is not ready to meet his maker and face judgment."

"Tie them up." Peter ordered. Akiro, Sayid, and Kato set to work disarming the weapons and restraining them as Jacob and I stood guard over the Syrians while Hideki and Peter guarded the door.

The Syrian who had not pulled his weapon inquired, "Are you the one, the one they speak of, the female warrior of Allah?"

I made no reply and he continued, "It is said that you have the strength of his arm, the speed of his spirit and you hear his voice from on high. Is this true?"

I did not know how to respond, I did not even know that this area of the world knew my story. I also had not heard the voice of God for so long now, he was silent, but I was compelled by the spirit within me to give this poor soul an answer. I took a moment and looked down at him with compassion as I replied, "I have been blessed with, strength, speed and agility by our creator and yes I have heard his voice, you are fighting on the wrong side in this war."

The Syrian beside him inquired, "Is it true you died and went to Paradise?"

I looked toward Jacob and he nodded slightly so I answered them, "Yes I died, and I went to Hell and back and then I entered Heaven and now I live again."

The Syrian who had pulled the gun on me before had changed in his spirit. His eyes lost all fear and they were filled with arrogance as he said, "This is impossible, it cannot be true. If you really are a warrior of Allah and can hear his voice show us. Prove yourself to be so."

"Hmm... same tricks snake. Some things never change. It is written, 'Trust in the LORD your God and depend not on your own perception.' Believe what you will Syrian." I replied as I looked toward the other captive and then back toward the one who questioned me as I ordered, "You snake, you remain silent. Speak no more."

The Syrian with an evil grin laughed, "Catherine you should know you have no authority, nor power over me."

I looked in the Syrian's eyes and saw the Devil's eyes and I ordered him one more time, "Be silent."

He laughed and I slid my knife across his side so that he would die slowly, I turned and questioned the other Syrian, "Do you want to truly live?" He nodded, yes.

"Then trust me and follow me, but before we leave this ship, I must slice the chip from your hand. Agreed?" I asked him. He nodded his assent again. We all made our way toward the bow of the ship.

We met with Yuri and his men, who had accomplished their mission, but they were badly injured and Michael was not with him. Yuri said, "He died a warriors death, we were successful."

I touched Yuri's shoulder as my men prepared to head back to the submersibles below.

I took a deep breath as I realized what I must do. I took my knife from its sheath and prepared to remove the Syrians chip. I would have to slice it from his hand and placed it in my own, knowing they could track the Syrian's movements once he disembarked and I was determined to take the Syrian with us.

"Catherine, what are you doing?" Peter inquired, but after realizing my intentions he yelled, "NO!"

"We need time. Seven seconds is not enough for you to escape. I will slice it from my hand after you all are free from enemy waters and then I will join you." I knew Peter would resist my decision, but I was compelled to continue in this.

"Damn it Catherine, You don't have to do this. Don't be a fool. This is not part of the plan. We did not save Sayid only to lose you into the enemy's hands. It is too dangerous and we don't need the Syrian anyways." Peter pleaded.

"There is no time to argue Peter. We saved Sayid and now we are saving this Syrian too. I will not leave him behind. The plan has changed now depart and I will join you later." I could tell Peter wouldn't leave me, so I ordered Jacob, "Take him with you. Go now!"

"Catherine this is ludicrous. It makes no sense."

"Peter, enough. I will give you the time you all need to get safely back to shore." I insisted. Then I kissed him and said, "I love you, trust me I will see you again. I've seen it."

They escaped and were far from the ship when I sliced the chip from my hand. I heard the alarm ring. It was not long before I was surrounded by Augustus' forces, the alarm went off too early. They must have discovered the men we killed before. They seized me. I was taken into custody and placed in chains. I was not afraid. I smiled because Peter was safe, Sayid was free and the Syrian had a chance to save his soul.

*****

Chapter Nine: Sacrifice

I don't know why, but I didn't resist arrest, I was confident that I could have escaped. Had I dove into the sea they would have never captured me, but I didn't resist, I just stood there frozen in place like some strange power held me there. I couldn't move and I didn't know why, but I was filled with peace and contentment knowing the people that I loved and cared about were safe.

I was brought to the same room where they held Sayid and I was tied to a chair in the brig. My ankles were fastened each other and my arms were chained together behind my back. A Syrian Captain came in and slapped me across the face and slapped me again with a back hand as he yelled at me in Syrian.

I jeered, "This might work better if I could understand what you're saying."

The Syrian interrogator spit at me and punched me in the face. Then he said, "You Americans are so cocky. You will regret ever sneaking aboard my ship."

I just grinned and said, "Your ship, I don't think Augustus would be pleased with such a statement, let alone Lumen."

He cuffed me in the back of the head and said, "Shut up. You will only speak when I tell you to."

He paced the floor in front of me and began to swing a baton as he said, "Now how many of you are on my ship? Who helped you in your sabotage of my nuclear missiles?"

I smiled slightly and said, "It's just me, there is no one else."

He hit me in the stomach with the baton and yelled, "Don't lie to me. Who else is with you? Who killed my men?"

I keeled forward and then I slowly sat up straight as one of my shorter layers of hair fell from my braid and covered half of my face and I taunted, "Now there you go again, calling them your men. Lumen would not be pleased; doesn't everything belong to the New World Order, to that poor excuse for a god." I shook my head as I watched his fury with me escalate as he backhanded me again in the face.

The Syrian Captain said, "Answer my questions, now who are you?"

I answered, "Well I am not an American, I can tell you that much."

He hit me with his baton again this time in my arm and said, "Who are you?"

I grimaced, but I said nothing.

He calmed himself and regained his composure and warned, "This is going to be a very long night for you and your efforts were in vain, my men will have the missiles ready by morning. Still you will suffer greatly before this night is through."

I laughed slightly, but said nothing. He did not know that even if he managed to fix the weapons they would not launch, thanks to Yuri. I remained silent.

He advised, "The pain will only increase if you do not cooperate, so for your own sake, tell me who you are and who else is with you?"

"I told you, I'm alone." I answered honestly.

"Impossible, you are only a little woman you could not have killed my men, who is with you?" The Syrian scoffed.

I said nothing in reply and then he declared, "Well if torture is the only way we can get you to tell us what we want to know, then torture it will be. It is a shame you are really quite beautiful, but it is the path you have chosen. You leave me no alternative."

He walked toward a table filled with various implements. He examined them as he informed me, "I confess, I have not had to torture anyone for many years, but since my chief interrogator is now dead, the responsibility falls to me. Still, I was once very skilled at this and I must say that I rather enjoyed it." He admitted as he grinned wickedly.

I didn't relish the thought of torture, but I did not fear it either. He was studding my reaction with a hint of disappointment and he was astonished that I was surprisingly calm.

He prepared a series of blades on a table before me and he heated a long iron rod that looked like a branding tool. He lifted one of my knives that had been confiscated; they had not found the other three for they did not search me for weapons, a foolish mistake that they would soon regret.

He lifted my knife off the table and examined it as he walked closer to me and he observed aloud,

"This is a beautiful throwing knife, but I don't think you could have used it on my men. No, no, I believe that you had help, but whom, who had the power to kill my men?"

I said nothing so he continued, "Hmm, well it is a lovely blade. Shall we see how sharp it is?"

He motioned to the guards, who then unchained my arms from behind me and fastened them to a chair. Then my torturer lifted my sleeve a little and slowly slid the blade along the length of my forearm. The blood flowed like a stream, still I gave little reaction, but I clenched my fist and took a long deep breath.

He stood up and examined me as he noted, "That is very surprising my dear and very impressive. You did not cringe, or cry out loud, perhaps you are a cutter. Are you used to such pain?"

I gave no reply and he said, "Hmm, or perhaps we did not cut deep enough." He moved suddenly and stabbed my hand through to the chair.

I swore out loud as I yelled, "Ahh! You fucking snake." Then I spit at him.

He grinned and raised one eyebrow, "Well, we have a reaction, but not the one I was hoping for. Curious, don't you have any fear? Perhaps I have lost my touch; I use to be quite a gifted interrogator."

I took another long deep breath as he reached for the hot iron and questioned me again, "Who are you? What are you?" He burned my other forearm. I clenched my fist; still, I did not utter a word. It hurt so badly. I wanted to scream and then I wanted to kill him, but I did neither. I just closed my eyes and breathed deeply and slowly ignoring everything else around me. I opened my eyes and he studied me again as he stated, "You intrigue me little lady, perhaps you don't truly feel pain."

I did not tell him that I did. I bore a child, I know what pain is, but I would not break. I would not crumble before a serpent like him. I couldn't give him the satisfaction. Then I sensed my Lord strengthen me from within as well. I felt my body healing; almost as quickly as the pain set in, it began to diminish. I smiled again.

He was perplexed by my reaction so he shared, "Well my dear, few can withstand torture as you do, with exception to our God's soldiers…" He said as he studied me and then concluded, "… but I don't think you are one of them. No, you would be taller, stronger and less defiant I think. So what are you and what do you fear?"

I grinned again and shook my head. I was truly unafraid and I believe I was filled with the spirit of God. I could feel his power, his resolve and his presence and then I felt a darker presence nearby as the Syrian said, "You are a women. I will find out if you feel anything at all. I will see if your fear what all women fear. I will have my way with you and then, so will each of my men."

He ripped my outer shirt open and saw the cross burnt into my flesh and he stumbled back and gasped. I had on a muscle shirt, but it was low enough to reveal the cross that Brother John had given me many years before. I looked at him and glared as he stared down at me dumbfounded.

I glared at him as I warned him in a cold tone, "If you try to violate me, I will kill you and each and every man on this ship."

As I uttered this threat Satan entered the room and he laughed, "She would too."

The Syrian bowed low to the ground before his god. The Devil walked toward me and leaned in as he inquired, "My queen, why didn't you kill him?" Satan brushed the hair out of my face gently and caressed my burn then continued, "Why did you allow him to mar your beautiful body?"

I glared at the Devil and I whispered, "Perhaps, I had mercy."

The Devil laughed, "I too can have mercy child." Satan pulled the knife from my hand and he watched as my hand as it healed instantly before him. "Your power is growing; soon you can rule with me, like a goddess by my side."

The Syrian begged, "Forgive me Master Lumen, I did not know she was your chosen vessel, forgive me, please have mercy."

Satan turned and ran his finger along the blade and tasted my blood, He smiled at me pleased and then he walked toward the Syrian officer licking and cleaning his fingertips.

Lucifer stated plainly, "Mercy, just because I choose to have compassion on my queen, why do you think I would show you clemency?"

"Please Master..." The Syrian began to plead again.

I interrupted, "I am not your queen, I'm not your vessel and there is only one God, and you forget I know you and you will not share your power with any human."

"Yes my dear, this is true, but you are not a human, or haven't they told you? Regardless, I assure you, you will be mine. You always were my child." He declared with resolve and arrogance.

"Never! I am the Lord's." I replied.

"You are a child of Hell my dear, not Heaven. Why do you think Yeshua shares you with Peter? I will have you too. In fact I already have."

Satan sickened and enraged me; I hated him like I could hate no other. Just hearing him mentioning Peter's name made me wish I had the power to kill him. He took pleasure in my reaction as I hissed, "Liar."

I was not afraid of him, but he did not want my fear and he laughed and said, "You know me so well, so look into my eyes and tell me if I'm lying now. You are mine."

I didn't reply, so he turned his attention to the Captain still cowering, bowing low before him. Satan walked toward him and apologized, "I am sorry this weasel of man harmed you my dear, but for some masochistic reason, that I cannot fathom, you allowed it. Were you testing your abilities?" The Devil looked back at me with curiosity as he continued to question, "Why? Why would you allow such a weak mortal to harm you, when you could have easily slayed him?"

I did not answer him, he shrugged and inquired, "No matter, would you like me to have mercy upon him my dear?"

"Unlike me, he is yours; you will do with him what you choose." I stated as a matter of fact.

Satan laughed out loud and then he turned toward his servant bowing low to the ground and gently placed his hand on the Syrian's shoulder. As the Captain sighed with relief, the Devil used my knife to slice the Syrian commander's forearm, who cried, "Please master Lumen, have pity."

The Devil took the hot iron and burned the man's face, he screamed out loud, crying and begging for his master to stop. Satan responded, "Did you cease and show her compassion when she begged you to stop?"

"She never begged for mercy master. Please, I live to serve you alone." The Syrian commander cried out as tears streamed down his face.

Satan turned and looked back at me and I had no concern or compassion for the Syrian. I was cold and emotionless and the Devil smiled and said, "Every time I see you, I am even more impressed by you. Amazing, little has impressed me for so long now. Like your favorite god, I too am a great believer in an eye for an eye and this man may not have taken your life, but he has taken others so..."The Devil turned swiftly and used my knife to slit the coward's throat in a swift and beautiful motion.

Satan spun and side stepped just as the blood spilled forth out of his neck. Thus he avoided getting blood on his beautiful well-tailored suit.

I gave no reaction even though I admired the precision and fluidity of his actions. Satan wiped the blade clean and he laughed to himself, "How fitting, the blade reads justice." Lucifer chuckled slightly to himself and slid the knife into his jacket pocket.

Satan turned and ordered two demon warriors of immense size and strength to take me with them. He commanded, "Take her and follow me."

They moved toward me and the Devil warned them, "Be careful Allocen, she is probably more powerful than both of you and she can strike quite suddenly. She is a deadly viper." Allocen raised an eyebrow in disbelief and then a subtle grin of admiration crossed his lips. Satan turned and laughed at his own joke as he made his way up the corridor and to the upper deck where a chopper was waiting for us to depart.

I was nauseated by the audacity that he would think of me as a snake like him. I was nothing like him, but I was pleased by his limitations. He could only know and see what he was present to observe, or what his demons reported to him.

He and his demons were limited by their corporeal form. I knew he was not omniscient, nor omnipresent. Only God himself had that capability, but something had changed since I was last forced to suffer his presence. He now had the power to temporarily possess any of his servants and see through their eyes. I had to be careful.

I had changed as well; I was stronger, faster and even more agile. I healed quickly and I knew things without being told of them. I couldn't explain it, or put my finger on it, but I was not arrogant enough to delude myself into thinking I could possibly defeat these demon soldiers, or Satan on my own.

I saw how Jacob had struggled in hand to hand combat earlier. Still, I was pleased that their human hosts could still be killed and I knew that these demons required a host to move about our realm. They could possess a living creature, but I felt strongly that if no living host was nearby when the human host was killed, the demon would then be forced to return to the abyss.

I smiled slightly to myself and I prayed God would help me and keep my unit safe, especially my Peter. I thought, "Oh Peter, how I love you, how I miss you." I thought. I wish that I could tell Peter how sorry I was. I would when we reunited, but for now I was compelled to wait for the right time, for the right moment when I would strike at the heart of the beast.

I was flown to Italy and imprisoned in an ancient castle. I knew Eric would be tracking me. I activated my tracking device just prior to boarding the helicopter. I could not write this account for many days, so some of it may lack in detail. I don't know why I am writing it at all. I just know that I feel compelled to write it down.

I knew Peter would be fearful for me and enraged that the enemy had me in their grasp again. Peter would not stop until he found me and held me in his arms again.

******

It was just after dawn one morning when Augustus himself arrived with my breakfast. He placed the tray down and I looked up at him.

I was sitting cross-legged in the middle of the floor. I slowly stood up. Augustus was short for a man. He was my height and wearing his black military uniform.

He was unafraid of me and he motioned, "Please miss Miles sit, have some breakfast with me."

I sat, but I refused to eat or drink and he said, "I can assure you that it is not poisoned my dear."

He ate and poured himself some orange juice, while I watched intently as he continued to speak. "Miss Miles, you should really keep your strength up. You are Lumen's captive and there is no escape. Why would you starve yourself when it will only make you weak?"

I gave no reply and he shrugged, "As you wish. Do you mind if I continue to eat while we talk?"

I did not reply so he ate and then he observed, "You are smaller than I expected. Do you know how long my forces have hunted you? Your rebels have caused me so much grief. Yet Master Lumen, he is patient with you, and this perplexes me. Do you know that whenever reports came in about a rebel faction disrupting his plans he would kill anyone at nearby in a volatile rage, however when it was you who launched an attack, even the most detrimental and devastating, threating our agenda, he smiled with pride? It is very mystifying indeed. Can you tell me why that is?"

I answered, "Well it's obvious that he is patient with you too. Why?"

"Oh, my dear it is a long, boring story. I am more interested in you. Tell me, is it true that you have been to Hell and back?" He looked at me intently trying to read my expressions, since I refused to give him a verbal reply.

"I see that you are unwilling to share, so how about an agreement? I will respond to your inquiry if you answer mine." He challenged as he poured himself some coffee. I raised an eyebrow and he said, "Ladies first, ask me anything?"

"Why are you here Augustus?" I asked.

He smiled, "Curiosity, but also a wise man once said, 'Know your enemy and know yourself.' There is wisdom in this."

I responded, "You did not finish. 'Know your enemy and know yourself, and you can fight a hundred battles without disaster.' This hasn't proven true for you."

Augustus was pleased as he declared. "Very good my dear. I see that you have read Sun Tzu as well. I'm impressed and you are correct. You and your rebels have been a thorn in my side, so to speak."

I didn't tell him that I hadn't read Sun Tzu. I had just read the quote somewhere before, but Augustus didn't need to know that. I observed, "You're not possessed, so why do you serve the Devil?"

"First you must answer my question." Augustus insisted, "Are you human my dear?"

"I am... I am the daughter of two mortal parents."

He grinned and replied to my earlier inquiry. "I am human as well. Are you spiritually possessed by a divine power?" He studied me intently.

"You didn't answer the second part of my question, yet." I replied trying to delay my answer.

"Very well, I'll give you this." He smiled and then he continued, "If it is true and you have been to Hell, then you have seen the power of my Master. No one can stop him and that is why I serve him."

"I have been to Heaven as well and I know the power of my God. You're on the losing side, Augustus." I replied.

His tone was arrogant as he chided, "It does not appear to me from your current situation that you're winning."

"The war's not over yet, Augustus." I warned.

"You say my name with such disdain my dear. Do you think me evil?" He inquired.

"You serve Evil, thus you are evil." I coldly stated

He smiled, "You see the world in black and white Ms. Miles. An evil leader to some is a hero to others."

"You are no hero, you are a selfish narcissist, grasping for power. You know Satan has nothing, but disdain for you and humanity. What makes you think when he is done with you, he won't discard you like trash?"

"You utter such hurtful words, and after I have treated you with such respect, but you're right." He conceded and continued, "Still, I know my Master and despite his hatred for humanity, our relationship is more complex. Besides," Augustus placed a grape in his mouth and chewed it and then noted, "He doesn't hate you, but you're not human are you? What are you that he would have such affinity for you? I have been nothing, but honest with you Miss Miles, but I think that you are lying to me. That is not very Christian of you, my dear. So, why don't you tell me who you really are or what you are? " Augustus asked as he studied me closely. I said nothing.

He continued, "That's alright Commander you don't have to answer. I have my suspicions, but I am afraid I must test my theory. Forgive me this will hurt, but you gave me no choice."

Augustus pulled two knives out, a combat knife and an ancient dagger covered in strange markings that I could not read. He assured, "Don't worry my dear I'm not going to kill you. This is just a test."

"Aren't you worried that I will kill you?" I challenged.

"Your reputation does precede you. I have taken precautions." Augustus smiled

Suddenly a whole host of demon mist like figures manifested themselves around me. Why hadn't I sensed them earlier? Then Allocen and another huge Demonic warrior entered the room.

"Augustus, what are you doing?" Allocen probed.

"A test, that's all. Please stay. I know that you are as curious as I am." Augustus replied.

He took the combat knife and sliced my forearm it healed immediately. Allocen grinned, and then he took the dagger and cut a very small knick on the inside of my forearm. It burned my flesh and it did not heal as quickly.

Augustus smiled, "You are not fully human after all? You're a half breed, a child of Hell and yet you serve Yeshua. Why?"

I said nothing and Allocen questioned, "You are Nephilim, don't you know that the Angels of God will hunt you down and exterminate you. You are an abomination to them. Why do you fight for them?"

The other Demon warrior spoke up, "This is impossible, the bloodlines died out millenniums ago. It cannot be."

Allocen replied, "Nothing is impossible. How many of you exist? Are you the only one, or are there more?"

I did not answer and Augusts said, "Thank you for your time my dear. Our visit has been illuminating. Allocen come with me."

Allocen said to the demons, "Find a host and increase the guard on detail." With that the demons in my room that had surrounded me vanished and they left me alone with my thoughts.

*****

Peter told me what had occurred after they departed the ship. They waited for me for some time, but when I did not follow them, they knew that I was captured.

I activated my beacon; however Eric was unable to track it right away. There was something jamming it, so they couldn't calculate my direction.

Peter was enraged and he took his fury out on the Syrian whom we rescued from the enemy. Peter hit him several times and said, "Where would they be taking Catherine?"

The Syrian replied, "I don't know, please believe me, I would tell you if I could."

Peter hit him again and said, "Don't lie to me, where would they take her?"

I fear Peter would have beaten the poor boy to death had Sayid not restrained him, "Peter enough! The boy doesn't know and Catherine would not have wanted you to harm him. We must find another way."

Peter ordered, "Get John, Eric and Sky back here. NOW!"

It was not long before they arrived and they held a meeting in Tel Aviv. "Eric, have you been able to locate Catherine? Where have they transported her to?"

"Unknown, I tracked her leaving the ship; however her signal was lost almost as quickly as it was activated." Eric replied nervously.

"Find out everything you can as to where they are likely to take her and Eric, this is your only priority." Peter took command even though the other commanders where there. Everyone understood the situation and said nothing.

Peter turned and glared at John and Jacob and he spoke to them in a harsh tone, "You both claim to have the ear of God and you both profess that you can hear his voice, it's time to prove it. God did not protect her before and if he is real than have him protect her and tell us where she is."

John replied gently, "Captain Roberts, Peter, a man cannot dictate to God; we petition, we have faith and trust in him, but he is not one we can make demands of, nor judge him. He alone is God."

Peter had no patience for religious lectures, "Is he God or not? Is he all powerful?"

John replied, "Yes, he is."

"Is Catherine his daughter?" Peter questioned.

Jacob paused and John answered, "Yes, she is."

Peter glared at Jacob and ordered, "Than tell him to act like it. He surely is a better father than I would be, and I would protect and save my child. If he is real and is who he claims to be, than as a father he has a duty to protect her, and from what I have heard Jacob, so do you."

"Yes I do Peter, but she still has free will. She has the freedom to make her own choices and she must deal with the consequences of her decision. I cannot protect her from the cost, or the sacrifice, required to pay for the path that she has chosen. I can only protect her from attack. My abilities and conditions of service to her are limited."

Jacob sighed knowing Peter could not understand and he was not at liberty to tell him the details of his service. He was my guardian angel, but Peter still viewed him as man.

"Convenient rationalizations for the limited nature of your god. Is he God or not? Can you speak to him and hear him?" Peter challenged.

"Yes Peter, but watch your tongue, for you are walking a very fine line." Jacob warned.

Peter heard a wrath in Jacob's voice tempered only by his love for me, but Peter abandoned any form of respect or patience and spoke harshly as he ordered, "Then ask him where they have taken Catherine, if he won't save her from her choice to sacrifice herself for others, than I will."

"As will I" said Sayid, "She sacrificed herself to save me; I will do the same for her."

Yuri added, "I will go too, she is too wonderful and unique a creature to leave in the enemy's hand."

Yamomoto added, "I fear she battles the Dragon himself and many demons, but I cannot let her face them alone. I too will go. My nephew Akiro and I are trained to fight the demons that we must now face."

Peter questioned, "What do you mean?"

Jacob answered, "Yamomoto and his lineage are from a very long line of demon slayers. They have not had to face them for generations."

Sayid said, "You wanted proof of the spiritual realm Peter, I am afraid you shall soon have it and encountering such evil can destroy almost any mortal."

Peter was un-phased by Sayid's warning, but he said, "Thank you all for you willingness to sacrifice yourselves to rescue her." Peter knew that I would do the same for any of them.

Now he had to find out where they were holding me and for the first time, Eric was blocked at every turn. He could not lock onto me and then he finally got a brief reading and he said, "Peter I got a brief locating beacon for Catherine, but I only know that she is somewhere in Italy, near Petiole. Sorry it was a very short signal; if I slept I would have missed it."

Peter patted Eric's back, and said, "Thank you Eric you did great. You can sleep on the plane."

Yuri noted, "What shall we do with our Syrian prisoner?"

Sayid answered, "Bring him with us, Catherine did not save him to leave him in Israeli custody."

Sayid asked, "Syrian, what's your name?"

The Syrian replied, "Matthias."

Peter warned, "Well Matthias, betray us, or betray Catherine's trust and you will die."

Matthias swallowed, but said nothing as they boarded the aircraft, destination Italy.

******

Chapter Ten: Angels and Demons

On the flight Peter overheard John and Jacob speaking with one another and John inquired, "Jacob you're not human are you?"

Jacob answered honestly, "No, I am not."

"Are you an angel?" John continued to question.

"Yes I am. I am Catherine's guardian." Jacob answered

John questioned, "How is it that we can see you, but not other angels?"

Jacob replied, "When an angel walks the earth he is in his human form, sometimes people recognize us, other times they don't. Our perceived visual presence in your realm is only upon the orders and allowance of God. We rarely expose ourselves to this dominion."

Peter turned, and challenged, "And why is that Jacob?"

Jacob looked up, as if briefly communicating with Heaven and then he responded, "Because our presence, our influence, could alter the outcome of human history and we are forbidden from interfering with the divine plan and human destiny."

Peter said, "You supposedly interfered with human history and destiny when your kind destroyed

Sodom and Gomorrah or chose a nation's side in various wars throughout history. Didn't you?"

"No we don't Peter, we correct it, rectify and return the balance, so that man can choose his own course. Sodom, Gomorrah, and ancient Babylon were under the influence of legions of demons. Their people were possessed in large numbers by a darkness that consumes them, rules them until no part of human choice, or dignity remains. "

Jacob was compelled to help Peter understand, but everyone on the plane was listening intently as Jacob spoke, "You see Peter, you may have heard it said that the Devil wanders the earth seeking whomever he may devour and this is true. He wants to destroy mankind; he hates them because God loves them. He also feels the earth is his because he was cast down here from the highest Heaven when he rebelled against God. He was livid when God gave the earth to mere mortals to tend.

Satan is evil, but he is still a prince in this world. Like the kingdoms of men there are good princes and evil ones. Jesus is the Prince of Peace, but on the cross he won this world and reclaimed it. He is the King of kings."

Peter spoke plainly, "Well, where is he then? He rules like an absentee landlord whose properties are in disarray. This world is in chaos Jacob."

"It is in chaos, and when the King returns, he will bring order to the chaos just as he did at the beginning of creation. Until then, he leaves it to the stewards of men to rule and reign, and they have done a very poor job of it." Jacob replied.

Jacob continued, "Satan had many legions of angels follow him when he tried to make himself equal to God, those fallen angels are known as demons. Some are very powerful, while others are weak. Some are more cunning than others and, like all of creation, each demon and angel has strengths and weaknesses. We were each initially designed for a specific purpose.

Our two worlds collide and have been at war since that day and only sometimes is it obvious in the realm of man. As angels we obey God and perform our functions following strict laws and guidelines, but the enemy does not always obey God, Satan and his minions constantly take opportunity to wreak havoc in this realm and the Devil endeavors to rule the earth again.

Demons can only possess a man if he allows them to enter in, usually through sin, perversity, and evil covenants, but the individual must also be open and unoccupied. That is why a true Christian cannot be possessed; they have the Holy Spirit of God inside them. The house is already filled, but if it is an empty vessel a demon can enter in and even legions of demons can share the same host. However, they are like parasites, they destroy not only the soul of the person; they eventually destroy the body as well.

When a demon takes residence in a person, or creature, the host is exceedingly strong, fast and few can stand against it. It is the same for angels when we enter this world, our powers, given by God are immense and powerful. We have far greater speed and ability on Heaven's side, but compared to humanity we seem invincible, we are not.

The longer we stay in the human world the weaker we become, we can still be stronger and faster than most men and we have knowledge few humans ever attain, thus we have less limited existences than an average man, but we know our power diminishes the longer we stay. My own strength is already waning. An angel's stay is usually strictly limited by God and we never experience such weakness."

"Then how do you know this is the result?" Yuri asked

John added, "Is that what happened in the days of old, where the myths of the ancient gods ruled in the ancient worlds and the legends of angels and demons came from?"

Jacob nodded, "Some of them, yes, and they enjoyed mankind's awe of them. Men worshiped them as gods and they did not turn from such adulation."

He added, "There was a time when angels walked the earth more freely. Many of the angels and the demons loved the human form, the pleasures of food, wine, and even woman were too much for many to deny."

John interjected, "Is that where the demigods came from, when the scriptures say that, "The sons of God slept with the daughters of men?"

Jacob nodded again, "Yes, the giants of old looked much like me; their offspring were larger, stronger, faster, and more knowledgeable than the men around them. They were in touch with both realms. They became, corrupt, proud, and too powerful and they began to rule over mankind, who was designed to be free."

Sky who had been silent for the entire trip spoke up, "Are their descendants spirit walkers?"

Jacob nodded again, "The demigods were destroyed and a few in their genetic line remained, but they are very rare. There have been seers, prophets, shaman, miracle makers, magicians, sages, demon slayers and warrior kings throughout the ages that descend from these two groups. All forms of witchcraft, seeing, magic were both feared and forbidden by early man. Some in the ancient world where viewed as oracles, they got their information from the demonic realm, but others were children who came from a line of love and they got their information and knowledge from God.

On this side of the cross Jesus did not only save you from sin and inhabit those who believe in him with his Spirit, protecting you from demon possession, he enables all who receive him to hear from and receive divine guidance, thereby restoring the balance to humanity. You can be truly free."

Peter sat back and closed his eyes, he did not know for sure, but he thought Jacob was going a little mad. His stories were far too outrageous for Peter to believe. He muttered, "Why is it that every time man does something extraordinary, unlike the average man, they attribute it to the gods, creating myths to explain their great feats?" Peter shook his head and uttered, "Fantasy, it is all nonsense."

Jacob said, "You are young Peter; you are but a man. You weren't there, so I understand why you find it hard to believe, what is history for me is a matter of faith for you."

Peter opened his eyes and laughed, "Of course I wasn't there and neither were you. None of us were, so how could you say such things are true?"

John was watching Jacob intently and mused, "But you were there, weren't you Jacob? This really is a matter of history for you."

Jacob answered honestly, "Yes, I have been in existence for eons. I have witnessed the entire history of mankind. I was given charge of Catherine when she was born, but I was only ordered to reveal myself to her when she entered the Rocky Mountains a few years ago."

Jacob shared, "Catherine was the only human in this generation to be given the living water to drink. Her strength and power through Christ will only grow and increase the longer she remains on earth. While my strength will diminish the longer I stay, but she will be safe, soon she will be stronger and faster than me."

Peter scoffed, "I thought you told me that she was a decedent of the Nephilim and that is why she is so powerful."

Jacob answered without offense, "She is, but when she was in Heaven she also drank the water from the fountain of life. I know you don't believe she really died Peter, but she did."

Akiro interjected, "Legend has it that my ancestor was brought to a great fountain and given water to drink, and he and his seed would be granted sight, health, speed and agility for as long as they upheld the Samurai code."

Hideki added, "Yes it is why you, Akiro are the best martial artist in the world and why age has little effect on me, but what runs through our veins is diluted compared to our ancestors."

Kato spoke up, "Legend has it that in the era of abundant chaos the Great Red Dragon had his brothers mate with humanity and formed a powerful and evil race that was taught the black arts. They lorded their power over the simpler races and then a group of White Dragons that descended from the skies and created their own race to destroy the evil line and end the era of chaos. A single family line from each remained since the Red dragon could not be destroyed nor his children who went into hiding. A powerful Silver Dragon emerged and gave one of the White dragon's decedents Living Water, this family is yours Master Yamamoto?"

Yamamoto replied, "Hei"

Sky spoke up, "My family has a similar legend, my ancestor was taken up the mountain and given a drink from a spring by his Creator and the Great Spirit promised to speak to him and through his descendants as well. I am the first in my generation to have no vision, to have no powers. It is why I left my tribe. I was sent on my vision quest when I came of age, but I had none. I could not face my people so I left, I was too ashamed."

Jacob placed his hand upon Sky's shoulder and assured him, "You do have that living water flowing through you Sky, however you don't see it. You have seen the cures to illness and disease others miss; you have been given insight into the genetic DNA of man. This is no coincidence. You too are gifted by God. Each is given, according to their faith, their walk and their destiny."

Yuri asked, "So Sayid, what is your story, next to Catherine and Akiro you are the best fighter among us why is that?"

Sayid looked ashamed as he replied, "I don't know my story, and neither did my father. Grandfather said that my father was a fool for moving to the land of the infidel, he would not share the blessing with my dad, and when he discovered that I married a Christian and served in the American army, he said that I betrayed our honor, destroyed our heritage and forfeited the immense blessings of Allah. The only thing I had of my heritage is the Qur'an."

Yuri shook his head and sighed, "And I thought Russians were harsh."

Sayid smiled as he said, "Catherine told me that God, Allah is Love and that he is far greater than the narrow doctrines and religions of men and that I am truly blessed by God. I believe this, I have always enjoyed his blessings and felt his hand upon me."

Eric smiled as he fondly recalled, "She told me something similar when she read to me from a book that contained every account of the teachings of Jesus. I believe it was in the book of Thomas, when Jesus said to Peter, 'Until a woman can be like man and a man become like a woman, he cannot enter into the kingdom of God.'

The human sexual form is irrelevant in Heaven. We are spirit, we live in a body and we have a soul and a mind. When all are in agreement and balanced we find peace. She told me, 'Seek the truth in this and I will never be ashamed before God.' I believe this to be true, for I always knew I had a knowledge insight and intelligence, I never cultivated it on my own. I knew that he was my creator, and I give him the glory for all that I am."

Sky responded, "My people have a similar belief, we call it two-spirited people. Catherine told me once what she told you and said this is likely why there is no marriage in Heaven, the human form is a shell, a vessel but the spirit goes on. It is also believed by my people that, some souls are new others are old. They have experienced this realm before in another time and perhaps as another sex."

"Ah, reincarnation, I know many who believe this." Kato noted.

"So Eric, do you have any great ancestors?" Hideki inquired.

Eric was either too humble or too embarrassed to reply, so Jacob answered for him, "If you are open to believe the legend, Eric is a direct descendent of Merlin."

John said amazed, "Merlin the great magician in King Arthur's court? He had descendants?"

Jacob laughed, "Well he never married, but he had many. He was less moral than you John. He had a weakness too. Many think it was pride, but it wasn't. He knew where his power came from. Still, his great powers only passed through one bloodline and Merlin's mother was a Nephilim decedent."

Peter was still agitated in his spirit as he now challenged, "Eric, do you believe this shit?"

Eric shrugged and said, "I don't know what to believe, but I knew that I was a decedent of Merlin and my mother taught me science from a young age. She said that magic is really just science and truth that most people don't comprehend. I use to believe that all magic was simply science and illusion in conjunction with mind manipulation, but ever since I crossed over and electricity flowed through me, I 've been changed Peter."

"Changed into what, a Nephilim?" Peter challenged.

Eric said, "I have been growing smarter, seeing things even more clearly and... well maybe it is better if I show you." Eric manifested blue electricity to cross his finger tips and he manipulated where it went as it danced back and forth across his fingertips.

Then Eric shot a bolt from his hand onto Andrei's map book that he was looking at, setting it on fire.

"Chyort voz'mi!" Yuri's man, Andrei swore out loud as he jumped up from his seat and doused the flames.

Yuri laughed, "I guess you descend from the magician after all."

"Enough, enough of our families' myths, legends and magic tricks. Jacob, if you really are an angel, prove it now!" Peter uttered with frustration.

"How, won't you rationalize anything I do?" Jacob retorted.

"No, I won't. Do it in front of all of us, Spread your wings and fly away, do whatever it is you do. Go to heaven and then get your report on Catherine, find out where she is being held and come back to us so we can save her. Go on do it! Oh yeah, I forgot, you're in your human form and all angels don't have wings." Peter said sarcastically.

The discussion would have to wait as everyone prepared to jump from the plane when the red light came on signaling that they were over Italy.

Peter ordered, "Kato please tie up and restrain our Syrian guest." Then Peter turned toward the pilot and said, "Captain please bring our Syrian guest to the American flagship."

The pilot responded, "Yes sir."

Sayid added, "And Captain, make sure that you inform them that the Syrian, Matthias was saved by Commander Miles, and is not a prisoner, but that we would appreciate it if they kept him under constant watch until we return for him."

The pilot replied, "Understood Sergeant Sayid."

Jacob declared, "Peter, I will do as you request, prove that I am an angel. We will both jump from the plane together, I will fall with you from the plane without a parachute and we will descend at the same speed. We will each land, you with your parachute and me without. Then when our feet have touched the ground I will leave for Heaven and you will see me disappear. I will rejoin you and tell you where exactly they are holding Catherine, but you must wait for me to return before you attack, even if you find out through another means where she is. Agreed?"

"Agreed." Peter said cautiously.

The pilot announced, "We have reached the jump sight. Ten seconds to departure, bay doors open. Good luck."

They all jumped from the plane. Jacob remained directly across from Peter the entire fall. He even went upward with Peter when Peter pulled open his chute, even though Jacob did not have one. Peter told me that he saw a bright light like a shadow bathed in blue fire, in the form of extended wings extended from Jacob's body and lit the ground beneath them.

When they landed safely Jacob reminded them, "Find a safe place to hide and wait for me, I'll be back."

Peter looked perplexed as he stated, "Jacob I saw what looked like wings of light when you descended from the plane, I thought you said that you didn't have wings."

Jacob smiled and corrected Peter, "No, I said not all angels have wings. Wait for me! I'll return as soon as possible." With that Jacob spread out giant wings glowing with light and blue fire and then he vanished flying toward the sky.

Peter could not believe what he witnessed even though he knew it to be true.

Sayid asked, "Do you believe him now, Peter?"

Peter responded, "Well, I will admit that he is something more than human."

Sayid shook his head and folded up his parachute and left to survey the area.

John said, "Peter, he really is an angel, a servant of God. Believe in him, surrender to Jesus."

"I don't know if I can do that John, I have so many questions, I don't even like the Hebrew God. He is cruel and petty and Jesus is not like me. He is the Prince of Peace and I can't follow that. I believe God is creator, it is obvious that Jacob is something other than human, but how can I give my heart to a god I don't love, a god I don't know, and a god I can't trust." Peter answered honestly.

John placed his hand on Peter's shoulder and assured him, "I will pray for you Peter. You can't know God except through Jesus, so it is a leap of faith that only you can take. I can only tell you, God is love and that he loves you. Whether you choose to believe it or not is up to you. I must also warn you, if we face demons that Jacob spoke of, if we face the Devil himself than you and anyone here who is an empty vessel can be, and probably will be possessed. Then your free will may vanish and you can be used against us. You could be turned against Catherine herself."

"Never, I won't let him in, I won't surrender. I could never betray her." Peter declared emphatically.

Sayid broke them up and ordered "We must find a safe place to hide. We can save this discussion for another time. Move out!" Everyone picked up their gear and began to make their way to a forested region nearby.

Peter told me that they found an old abandoned church deep in a wooded region where they made camp and awaited Jacob's return.

As they sat around the fire John asked, "Peter, why do you find it so difficult to trust God?"

Peter stared at John and thought for a moment and responded, "I guess there are many reasons. I have never seen, heard or known him in any way. I grew up in America, where my only view of Christianity, was colored by exposure to corrupt politicians and business leaders that were nothing less than hypocrites and liars. They embraced greed, hatred and judgmental and divisive agendas, while proclaiming to follow Christ."

John looked sad and sighed, "I understand how difficult this is when Jesus taught, love, acceptance, inclusion, peace, feeding the hungry, healing the sick and walking away from materialism, and he literally ordered his followers not to judge."

Peter answered, "Exactly, and this Christian doctrine was a tool to manipulate the masses and get them to accept things with a fatalistic attitude. Quite frankly hypocrites and manipulation make me sick."

Yuri agreed, "Yes, it is no different in Russia. I understand; while the rich get richer and the poor and suffering grow with every passing decade. Greed, politics and religion don't mix... ahh." Yuri spit.

Sky said, "I know, whether it was the radical Islamists promoting suicide, hatred of the west and terrorism, or it was the radical Christian right, promoting greed and hatred against Indians and anyone not like them, there was little of God to be seen in the religions of men. Where was the Christ to be seen in Christianity, I could never see it either."

Peter added, "I learned very early in life that the religions of men was not only harmful to the human mind it was harmful to society at large."

Sayid weighed in too, "Everything you say is true, and Muslim extremists hijacked our religion, much like American politicians and Corporations and hate groups like the Arian Nations did with Christianity, to further their own interests, but you can't blame Allah for the evil these men do in his name."

Peter challenged, "Can't I? I don't know, if he really is God he allows it; he does not intervene to stop it. I know you will tell me that it is free will, Catherine and I have had many such discussions, but the fact is God , if he is God has failed to make this world better, his so called encounters with the human race has only led to division, manipulation, and an entire history of wars in his name. I don't believe in God as you all do, but Catherine and Jacob have shown me things that I can't explain, so I believe he exists in some form, but I don't know him..."

Peter stared off into the distance and continued, "However Catherine said one thing that I truly agree with."

John inquired, "And what was that?"

Peter answered in a calm, but cold tone, "She told me it was not her responsibility to save me; it was God's job. I believe that man should not struggle and wrestle to discover God, it is his duty to reveal himself to us, undeniably, beyond a shadow of a doubt and he hasn't. He hasn't even defended those who believe in him. He sure as hell didn't protect Catherine."

Sayid looks sad as he says, "Your thinking of Catherine and her incarceration, the beatings and the rape."

John declared, "Catherine told me that her experience in Hell and the insane asylum made her stronger because she realized that she could endure physical beatings, and horrible torture, and that her spirit with Christ could never be defeated. In a strange way she was thankful for that realization."

"Bullshit. When those bustards raped her, it nearly destroyed her." Peter raged.

Sayid added, "But it didn't Peter. She told me something similar and she said her love for you, the hope of one day being your wife helped her survive her greatest fear, rape. She knew if she could mentally survive that ordeal, she could survive anything."

Peter had a tear in his eye as he countered, "I know Sayid, but a child of the highest god should not have to fight to survive, he should defend them, and protect them. They should thrive and be better than any enemy they face. No, he fails his so called children constantly, but I can no longer deny he exists, I just can't trust him, if I had his power, I would never allow anyone to harm her, let alone violate her. How the hell can he?"

Sayid sighed, "It is hard to understand the mind of Allah, but he has equipped her to protect herself. Most cannot do the things she is capable of, and her powers grow with each passing day, you have seen this brother."

"It doesn't change the fact that he didn't protect her before and he has allowed her to fall into enemy hands again, Sayid." Peter seethed with anger as he gritted his teeth in reply. He was too enraged to speak and silence fell as the squad struggled with their personal thoughts and fears and internal spiritual struggles.

*****

Meanwhile I was not tortured physically and I was not bound, but my room had no escape and the Devil tried to play mind games on me. How I hated him. I knew he would not stop trying to turn me against God.

Satan sat back in a velvet chair across from me and asked, "My dear, why are you loyal to a god that abandons you and leaves you in the hands of his enemy. He allows you to sacrifice yourself, your body and your freedom for what, for the privilege to be able to bow before him and jump at his command. Is worshiping him really worth such a sacrifice of self?"

I gave no reply so he continued speaking, "He is the one who is cruel, he made you beautiful, men desire you, many adore you, they are even willing to lay down their lives for you, but he wouldn't even allow you to enjoy the pleasure of their most intimate expressions of that adoration.

John loves you and you love him and yet it was consider a sin for him to express that love. He should have been your first."

I looked up and noted, "That is a different kind of love and you know it. You were trying to use our friendship to claim my soul and destroy his. You don't fool me Lucifer; you were simply waiting for me to tempt him so that he would fall. Why?"

Satan grinned, "I know you too well, my child. You were right in saying that you were misname. I assure you, I had nothing to do with the temptation of Brother John. That was all you my dear, but I enjoyed watching. You are a sensual creature starving for satisfaction. I could give you that in way you could not even imagine, if you dared? Would you like a glimpse?"

He tried to place a picture in my mind, but I took it captive and spit at him, "Don't try to enter my mind! Leave me!"

The Devil laughed and said, "You are so proud and arrogant child, you presume you have the authority, the power to order me." He laughed, "Such audacity." Then he placed his finger under my chin and added, "You should be thankful that I find your belligerent nature amusing, my dear. I have killed others for less than that."

I moved his hand away and I declared, "You don't have any say in whether I live or die, my life is in God's hands."

The Devil smiled and said, "There you go again, so much presumption." He said with a subtle hint of pride as he turned to pour a glass a wine and he took a sip and continued, "There is so much that you don't know. You are now in my territory, my realm of power and influence and I made you my prisoner when you decided to remain on that ship. I have more power than you could fathom. I assure you, I have the power to destroy you, your life is in my hands and you should be more appreciative, I want you to live, child."

He took another sip of wine enjoying both the bouquet and the flavor immensely and he fished his wine and said, "At least I want you alive for now and I have enjoyed ravishing you more times than you have known." He said as his finger caressed my chin and down my neck.

"You're a liar!" I snapped as I moved his hand away and tried to twist his arm. He swiftly reacted, anticipating my move and twisted my arm behind my back.

He was such a deceiver; how I wished I could destroy him, but I knew that was the Lord's job alone.

The Devil whispered in my ear, "My dear, you know the man you have chosen to be your husband is an empty vessel, whom I have inhabited many times, especially when he lay with you." He kissed my neck and turned me towards him.

I could not help, but strike at him. He dodged my hit with ease and grasped my wrist again. I warned, "You leave Peter out of this you lying snake."

"I could leave him out of this, but he is coming for you soon. It is the beauty of free will my dear, he too has already made his choice. I may choose him as a vessel for my favorite demons, he is a lot better a choice then your sniveling brother was. The legions are thankful for a home, but Peter... yes he is proud and arrogant like you. I enjoy breaking such men, making them weak to do my bidding. My legions would appreciate that host."

The Devil knew my weakness, but I knew my God, I have prayed daily for protection over Peter and I knew my God honored my prayers and answered them. He would not only protect Peter he would reveal himself to him when the time was right.

Peter and I were one and nothing, especially this lying viper, could ever separate us from that love. Peter was a part of me and he was blessed and protected because of that union and the faithfulness of God. I had to control my tongue and ignore the Devil and not engage him. Yet, I was compelled to resist him.

He still had me by the wrist. He smiled, released me, stepped back and laughed, "Physically your powers are growing child, but you forget I don't need to rely upon my physical powers alone."

Satan grinned as I felt a powerful force enter my being and grasp my lungs while pulling me to my knees.

The Devil warned, "Be careful my dear, for I don't even require a word to kill you, all I need is a thought, an inclination."

I ignored the pain and prayed silently. I felt his grasp wane and I could breathe again. I stood up and Satan instantly threw me across the room and I landed on the bed. I struggled to get up but he forced my body down as he sat across the room.

I was enraged and I made a picture fly across the room toward him. He smiled and sent it back through the air to its original position on the wall.

He laughed "No, my dear I am rather fond of that piece of art." It was an oil painting of a woman being seduced by a demon.

I responded by having it spontaneously ignite and burn.

Satan walked toward me leaned over and kissed my lips. I tried to turn, but his power was too forceful. "My dear you are a tenacious thing aren't you. I could have killed you my child, I told you that I liked that painting, but I am rather fond of this side of you, so yet again, I am going to have mercy on you. He kissed me again." He laughed and then got up and left the room locking the door behind him.

I was released from his power and I screamed in rage.

I refused to eat or drink and it had been three days since I had either food or water, but I knew the food and drink was likely to be drugged, so I partook of neither.

****

Meanwhile my men in the church fell asleep as they awaited Jacob's return.

Peter awoke suddenly with a start. Eric, John and Hideki were up already, while everyone else remained in a deep slumber.

Sayid awoke with a start shortly after Peter.

Hideki placed his hand on Peter's shoulder and remarked, "You slept deeply Peter."

Peter replied, "Yes, but I had awful nightmares."

John inquired, "Nightmares of Catherine being beaten, tortured and raped?" Peter nodded and John lamented, "I had the same dream."

Hideki cautioned them, "Pay no mind to them; it is one of the Devil's tricks."

Peter declared, "It's been three days already. We must save her. We can't leave her to suffer, not again, we must rescue her now."

Hideki said, "We must wait. Be patient, we don't even know where they're holding her."

Peter rose and paced as he asked, "What's taking Jacob so long?"

Eric had discovered where I was; he had picked up my beacon again. Eric said, "I just got a signal. I know where she is."

They wanted to rescue me right away. Peter was emphatic as he insisted, "We must go save her. We can't leave her to suffer, not this time. Eric, tell me where she is."

John reminded Peter, "We must wait for Jacob to return"

Peter scoffed, "Wait for what, for her to be brutally treated, and raped over and over again? No! We're already too late, but I won't leave her in their hands again, in his. We're going now! Eric where is she?"

John placed his arm on Peter and warned, "We must wait on God. We cannot defeat this enemy, or be of any help to Catherine without him. Please wait Peter."

John didn't know Peter well, but Sayid did and he cautioned and reminded Peter, "Brother, you have seen with your own eyes that which is impossible for man is possible with God. Jacob is indeed an angel of the Most High. We must wait on him. If you cannot yet trust Allah, trust Jacob; you know him. He will come soon. Peter, you gave him your word, remember."

Peter was a man of his word and Sayid knew that, but he appealed to Peter's rational too and added, "Eric do you have the schematics of the building in which she is held?"

"Yes" Eric replied feeling compassion for Peter's state of helplessness.

"Peter lets go over the schematics together while we wait and come up with a rescue plan." Sayid suggested and Peter nodded his assent.

Eric showed them the laptop as he said, "She briefly reactivated her signal; it originated here on the east wing and was turned off here in the center tower. It won't be easy. There is only one-way in and out."

Peter inquired, "Are the satellites in position yet? How many guards are there?"

Eric declared, "The satellite is coming into range now." Then Eric added, "It looks like there are two, one at each end of the wall and several near the actual entrance, but if we scale the wall here, there is only one walking the length of the wall."

Sayid pointed at the screen and said, "Okay we will take the guard out and then position you here

Eric, and you can snipe anyone who gets in our way. We will make our way inside and get Catherine through this entrance. You stay out of sight until we make our way back into the courtyard and then you can provide cover fire while we escape."

Peter said, "Demons or not they bleed and therefore can die. We will kill without hesitation, everyone we encounter, but we must do so as silently as possible."

Yuri asked, "We must move like ghosts ourselves. Should we wait for darkness so that we are less likely to be seen?"

Hideki said, "Night or day, it matters not, demons dwell in darkness, they will see us either way. They are likely to sense our presence before they see us and we them. It is somewhat inevitable. Our only hope is that they are distracted by the earthly pleasures of life."

John said, "They are likely to be preoccupied. They have not been in human hosts in such numbers for thousands of years. They are not known for their restraint and discipline."

Peter said, "Regardless, they will be expecting us, they know our reputations and character. They will be anticipating a rescue mission."

Sayid agreed, "True, they know there is nothing we would not risk to rescue Catherine."

Hideki added, "But they are proud and arrogant, they believe they are invincible and that mere mortals are of no consequence. They also assume we don't know where they are holding her."

Sky added, "My people have something like a medicine bag to keep demons or bad spirits from sensing you, but you need a powerful shaman to bless them, nonetheless we have a powerful mark as well that anyone can give themselves it looks like this." Sky took off his shirt to reveal a tattoo-like mark. It looked like a circle with a diamond shape in the middle and three feathers dangling.

John said, "I have a similar tattoo on my heart it is a circle with a pentagram on it. The entire sigil is surrounded by a Celtic chainlike circle." John revealed his tattoo.

Peter questioned, "John isn't that the devil's star? I thought you were Catholic."

John smiled, "I am a Christian Peter; this is an ancient symbol that contains the Hebrew name of God, Yahweh, on it. Actually, I need to correct myself, the form of an interwoven pentagram encircled in it is the Greek word for the name of God. This symbol is powerful in seeking divine protection. It's not evil."

"What about the Celtic cross on your arms what does that represent?" Peter inquired.

John answered, "I wear a Celtic cross, but I don't have a tattoo of it. It symbolizes the unity and flow between heaven, earth and the four elements."

Sky said, "Yes mine has a similar meaning in that we are all a part of the sacred circle and our creator unites and protects us."

"Hideki, what about you are you protected by some form of religious mark." Yuri asked.

"Yes we have a Japanese symbol that can be loosely translated, 'victory over evil.' It is on the back of our left shoulder."

Soku questioned, "What about you Commander Michaelovich, do you have any amulets or tattoos?"

Yuri laughed, "No son, I put no faith in such things, I put my trust in my gun. I shoot the bastards in the head. I have yet to see any get up from that." Peter laughed and then they all did.

John suggested, "Peter perhaps we should mark you as well."

Peter replied, "It wouldn't help, I don't believe in it. Besides which mark would I choose? No, John there is no point in it."

Eric suggested, "We could mark you with all of them, then you would be safe."

"Eric thanks for your concern, but I am pretty sure it doesn't work that way, if it even works at all."

Peter did not tell me exactly how long Jacob took to return, but he said to me later, "It felt like an eternity Catherine. Still the men tried to keep my mind off you. It didn't work."

Jacob suddenly appeared that morning with three other angelic beings by his side. Peter saw Nahor, Lazaro and a third tall strong Black Angel with eyes the color of amber. Jacob spoke, "Thank you for waiting Peter, you are a man of your word."

Peter looked a little sheepish and replied, "Don't thank me, thank Sayid; I would have left at dawn to rescue her."

Jacob placed a hand on Peter's shoulder, "You took wise counsel, but you still kept your word. Had you chosen badly, I can assure you, you would have failed and you would have died or worse."

"Where is John Raziel?" Peter inquired suddenly fearing his safety as well.

Nahor replied, "Raziel is safe; he is under the protection of the angels. We were sent because the balance has been severely disrupted, John Raziel insisted we help rescue his mother. Lucifer not only tampered with creation and made man stronger and faster, he has placed legions of demons inside them. The power of the enemy is growing with each passing day and mortals can no longer stand alone. We have come to fight in your stead."

"In our stead, what do you mean by that?" Peter demanded.

"Well men must fight..." Jacob replied, "...but not you. The Lord has requested you stand down, hide and wait for us to return." Then Jacob faced the other men and said, "You are all asked to enter into battle, but it is likely you will die, so the Lord warned that you must prepare your souls for death, before you wage war. He said you may lose your lives, but your sacrifice will secure Catherine's release."

Yuri bowed and turned to face John and they walked off together to pray. Sayid turned and went his own way to pray, as did Soku, Hideki and Kato. Andrei turned and followed toward John, Vladimir stayed behind and asked Jacob, "Am I still human, do I have a soul? I have been altered."

Jacob nodded and replied, "You may go and confess you have tampered with the Lord's creation, but you are still his temple and you have not lost your soul. Go prepare yourself." Vladimir bowed and went off with the others.

Peter questioned, "Why am I requested to stay behind? Why aren't I permitted to go and rescue the woman I love? Am I supposed to sit here and do nothing?"

Jacob answered plainly, "Yes, because you are an empty vessel, it is possible the enemy could take hold of you and possess you."

"I won't let him. I would never let evil enter in." Peter declared.

Lazaro stated, "You are not even truly convinced Satan is the Devil, the Prince of Darkness. How will you be on guard if you do not even acknowledge who he is? If you did believe, how would you, a mere mortal, fight against him when ordinary angels cannot defeat him? Peter you have no idea the power you wage war against."

Peter reasoned, "You're right, but if your all powerful and almighty god is limited by our lack of faith from intervening in our lives then how much more limited should his advisory be, when I refuse to believe in him? Don't you proclaim that he is weaker than your god? Doesn't the scripture say, 'Resist the Devil and he will flee?' ... Well doesn't it?"

Nahor cautioned, "Yes it does Peter, but the word is like a river that flows like one truth into the next. You cannot resist the Devil and win without the amour of God."

Peter prodded, "Well your bible also says that I need not worry for this is the Lord's battle and he is the defender of the weak. Who is weaker than an unbeliever according to the scriptures?"

Lazaro smiled, "Peter you are indeed insightful, but they are correct, without the Holy Spirit of God inside you, you are vulnerable to the enemy."

Nahor added, "Peter search your heart, you know that you are an empty vessel, and you can be filled. I know that you can sense this, you have felt the emptiness you're your entire life." Peter could not argue with Nahor and his words cut to the very heart of Peter's inner-self. Nahor placed his hand on Peter's shoulder and continued, "God honors free will. Satan does not. He has the power to fill you with every quality you despise. Heed God's warning and don't come."

Jacob cautioned Peter, "Peter you are a noble man, and even I have learned much from observing you. You are loyal, moral and generally you are wise, and honest, but the enemy is crafty and cunning. He is not known for giving his victims a choice. He only needs the smallest crack of a window open to enter in. You are not perfect, there has only been one who was perfect, and he had a hard time resisting the temptations of the Devil. He was the only one who was tempted in all things and did not sin. You my friend are not that man, you are not strong enough to battle Lucifer and win."

"And these men are? Who is strong enough?" Peter challenged.

Eric answered, "None of us are Peter, and we are all too weak in our own strength. Even though our walk with God is not perfect and our doctrines may be tainted, it is in Christ alone we place our faith. His Spirit dwells in every believer and evil cannot possess us."

John added, "Those of us who walk in sin instead of righteousness are crippled and lame, we may be oppressed by the enemy and the consequences of our choices are real, but anyone who believes on Jesus will be saved. He is the Savior and the King. Honor his request, for he would not give you this message without reason. Trust him, trust Jacob …"

Sayid returned from prayer and heard some of the conversation, so he placed a hand on Peter's shoulder and finished john's sentence, "…and trust us Peter, we will lay down our lives to save her."

Yuri added, "She will return to you. I promise. Wait for us, and stay behind my friend, pozhaluysta, please stay."

"Is the Devil bound by time and space, what makes you think that as soon as he realizes that I am not with you he won't send his legions here instead?" Peter reasoned.

Lazaro answered, "We don't know, but the Lord does and he has requested that you Sky, take Catherine's bow and defend Peter. Don't let anyone, any creature at all, no matter how small within twenty feet of him.

Peter your sword can be used to kill demons, but guard your heart and your thoughts, because if they are near they will provoke, pride, anger, rage, hate, judgment self-righteousness, resentment, and lust, anything to make you weak. Should any of these be turned toward God you will fall and you are already angry with the him.

Be careful and stay awake, Satan can attack you in your dreams as well. I wish you could trust the Lord, but at least be open to him. Ultimately it is only he who can truly save you." Peter nodded, but said nothing.

Jacob added, "Nahor, Lazaro and Arron here will be going to rescue Catherine, but we require one more volunteer to stay behind and protect Peter, should the enemy attack. I think this would be wise."

Kato looked toward Hideki who nodded in return, "I will protect the Captain."

Peter said, "Thank you Kato, thank you Hideki." He knew Hideki's men never left his side, they stood by him and protected him with their lives and now Hideki willingly gave a part of that protection to Peter. I would be eternally grateful to him for that sacrifice. Then he added, "Bring her back to me."

Hideki bowed and replied, "We will." With that, they all turned to leave.

Sayid faced John, "John you are a prayer warrior not a soldier, please stay here as well."

John agreed, "I will stay and pray for your success and protection."

Sayid replied, "Allahu Akbar."

Yuri inquired, "Sayid what does that saying mean?"

Sayid answered and informed them, "It means, 'Allah is the Greatest' or 'God is the Greatest.' We say it when wish to express our approval of what we hear and when we want to praise a speaker for uttering what pleases God."

John smiled and said, "While thank you and I agree. God bless you my brother. God bless all of you."

With that the men left and followed Lazaro and Arron who led the way. Nahor walked with the men and Jacob took up the rear. My men would have to battle demons, but at least they had the angels fighting with them.

*****

Chapter Eleven: In the Hands of God

Sayid told me that they walked much of the night and most of the day toward a castle, not far from their encampment.

They scaled the castle walls and climbed up past the east side just as darkness began to fall. They made their way to the center tower where I was being held. Eric remained on the wall where they entered high above the courtyard with his rifle and a silencer in hand.

He killed several enemies without even alerting any others. Our men would not have to face had to hand combat until they reached the inside corridors. As they made their way through the halls and corridors toward my room they fought two by two with the exception of the angels and Akiro who engaged in hand to hand combat alone. Sayid was paired with the Russian Andrei. Yuri and Vladimir fought side by side and Hideki and Soku fought together in the attack.

They did carry hand guns, but they did not fire them instead they stalked their prey silently and killed many of them swiftly with a knife. They did not have long, for the demons where released from the bodies and a green mist would slither its way down the hall and enter another host.

Arron declared, "The shedim do not have long to survive in this realm without a host, so they enter one as soon as possible, but a smart one will soon alert Satan of our presence."

Nahor said, "The fallen will look toward their own self-preservation before any duty to Lucifer."

Lazaro noted, "Brothers, you forget their fear of Lucifer's power and they are well aware of his vengeful nature. They know he will act against them maliciously, should they fail in their duty."

It was at this same time that three women arrived in my room to dress me in more ladylike attire. I broke the neck of one with ease and the second one I punched and crushed her trachea. The third ran to get the guards as green mist from the other two slithered slowly about the room seeking a host.

■■

The third woman returned swiftly with two large demon guards. The first of which warned, "You have been commanded to wash and dress appropriately for our master. Do so willingly or we will force you to comply."

I proclaimed, "If you try, you will die and you will find yourself back in the abyss." I thanked God that I was in my combat gear and that I still had knives hidden close to my body.

As the first soldier entered the room I grasped my knives and uttered, "Thank you Jesus." I threw two knives towards the larger ones throat. He pulled them out and blood gushed forth as the second rushed toward me. A red mist rose from the first soldier moving like a dense cloud.

The second demon soldier came at me swiftly and he threw me across the room.

I went crashing against a mirror. I got up quickly and looked down at the broken glass and then back toward the demon and said, "Bad luck for you."

He smiled and prepared to engage me in hand to hand combat. He said, "Let's go little queen, let us see how good you really are."

"I've killed many of your brethren, are you ready to go back to Hell too." I challenged.

He laughed, "I am going to enjoy this."

I was striking at my assailment with veracious speed. I moved with agility and maneuvered swiftly avoiding and redirecting most of his strikes. He moved to kick me with a snap kick, but I stepped back and to the side as I pulled the third knife from my side.

He mocked, "You don't look so tough, mortal. I will now crush you and show you your place in creation."

"Your boss should keep you more informed." I told him and then I moved swiftly and whispered in his ear as I sliced his throat, "I'm no longer mortal."

The demon mist from the first one I killed entered into the demon guard that I was fighting. I was sure the demon was too late. I killed his only vessel. The large demon was wide eyed and then his eyes turned red. The other demon entered in before the moment of death and was strengthening and healing the one that I sliced across the trachea.

I thrust my blade into his abdomen and removed it. It had little effect. It penetrated a thick wall of muscle, but it did not reach any vital organs.

The demon smiled and then he picked me up by the throat, he could have crushed my trachea, but he didn't, as I warned in a rough voice, barely audible, "You can't kill me."

The demon warrior smiled, "Shall we test that theory."

I choked out, "You could and what would Lucifer do to you if you succeeded?"

He glared at me. He hesitated, so I took the opportunity to lodge my knife into his throat. I twisted it and he released me.

I keeled over and caught my breath as the demons fled from the soldier at my feet and traversed down the hall. Jacob and Nahor were both standing at the door in front of me.

I ran up and hugged Jacob and then I asked, fearfully, "Where's Peter?"

Jacob answered, "He is at camp, He was asked not to come."

"Thank God" I replied and I informed them, "The Devil wants to lay hold of him; Satan knows that Peter is my weakness."

"We must return to him quickly; we don't have long. I am sure the demons are informing Satan of our arrival as we speak." Nahor warned.

As we said this, the woman who I had not killed earlier was hiding in the hall and she overheard what was said. She turned to inform her master.

Soku saw her too, as did Hideki and they both threw their throwing knives and they simultaneously penetrated the back of her skull. She collapsed to the ground and the demons where released and slithered their way down the staircase.

"We must hurry they will be sent to hunt after Peter." I uttered with a hint of desperation in my tone.

An alarm sounded. As we made our way into the courtyard Eric took out three more men in pursuit of us. I smiled my gratitude in his direction. He grinned and took out another soldier behind us.

We safely reached a staircase going up toward the outer wall. When we reached the top I sighed a sigh of relief my men where all unharmed.

I saw Eric smiling at us as we approached and he stood up to come and join us.

As he took his first step forward, from behind him a giant demon soldier approached. He lifted Eric off his feet and broke his neck with ease.

I screamed, "No!" I ran swiftly toward him. The soldier faced me without fear and Jacob and Nahor where right behind me. I kicked the demon with such force he flew off the wall and went crashing to the ground below.

Sayid and Andrei were fighting off another soldier on the wall while Hideki and Soku where fighting another on the stair case, both succeeded in killing their assailants, but they were exhausted, save the Russians, who were shooting the enemy between the eyes.

I sobbed as I held Eric to my chest and looked down at his lifeless body. I couldn't move as I wept bitterly. Akiro jumped over us as I held Eric in my arms crying, "No, no, not Eric Lord. I asked you to bless him. No."

Akiro took on another enemy combatant near me. He was fast and agile; this demon soldier looked pleased to be fighting Akiro. Akiro pulled out a blade and sliced the demon's throat with ease.

Then I remembered Peter. I wiped my eyes and stood up to see a hoard of warriors coming toward us and a legion of angels descended from the skies, in a blinding ray of sunlight. They stood with us on the castle walls. The arch angel Michael was by my side.

Arron said bowing, "My lord, I feared we had to face these Shedim alone".

"I was busy on another field Arron. I was confident that you could handle them until I arrived. You did not disappoint me, but you do look like you have your hands full."

Michael reached out his hand to me and helped me up. I smiled. "Catherine, I told you, I am never very far away."

"Hello Michael, Peter is in danger." I replied.

Nahor and Lazaro were engaged in a fierce battle below us when Michael whistled to them and they immediately turned and leapt up to join us.

The demon soldiers saw Michael and his army and ceased their advance immediately as Nahor, Lazaro and Jacob bowed and said in unison, "My lord."

Satan emerged from the castle keep and sauntered into the courtyard below us.

He ordered his minions, "What are you all doing standing around. Attack! Kill them!"

Satan's general Allocen stated, "Master, we have just begun to enjoy our caporal forms and you said we would have a swift and easy victory, but that woman and her soldiers kill us with ease. This should not be so, they are only human.

How is this possible? Now you want us to face Michael and his army. We will lose. I will not return to the underworld so quickly. Until you prove we can fight and win, I will not sacrifice my life so you can have that woman."

"How dare you defy me?" Satan replied as he took him by the throat and held him with his feet off the ground and crushed his general's throat with ease. He died and a red mist dissipated into the earth beneath his feet.

Michael said to Arron now standing at his side, "Our brother Lucifer has been busy. Not only did he raise an army to wage war on the Heavens, he has enough to battle us on earth too."

Lucifer warned the guards as he continued, "If you do not fight, his legions will destroy you anyways. You are not fighting to lay hold of the woman; you are fighting for your very survival. Now charge our enemies, or I will destroy you myself."

Satan looked toward another demon soldier and said, "Azazel, you have just been promoted; don't disappoint me!"

The commander bowed in obedience and led the advance against us while Lucifer smiled and watched his army prepare to confront his enemy. Just then I noticed another soldier come whisper in his ear and he smiled directly at me, turned and walked away. I knew he was going after Peter.

Michael ordered "You all flee! We will stay and fight. Go, go now!"

Jacob, Nahor, Lazaro and Arron took Soku, Hideki, Yuri and Andrei in their arms and jumped to the ground below. Vladimir, Akiro, Sayid and I quickly repelled down the wall behind them. We all then sprinted across the open ground toward the forest as the battle continued behind us. When we reached the wood we slowed to a jog and then very briefly stopped by a spring.

Jacob ordered me, "Drink deeply, you must drink before we can continue."

"I'm fine. We must get to Peter, before Satan does."

Jacob ordered again, "Drink." So I did, I knew he would not move until I was taken care of.

"We can move much faster than the humans. Let us go ahead and we will protect him." Arron suggested.

"Jacob you go too." I commanded.

"I must stay and protect you." Jacob replied.

"I am fine, protect Peter. Defend him and you are protecting me Jacob. He and I are one." I insisted.

"It doesn't work that way Catherine, I can't leave you. I was sent to guard you, not him." Jacob was adamant, but so was I.

"You can and you will. Now go protect him. Do not allow the enemy lay one finger on him. He is mine. I am nothing without him. Jacob, please." I would not relent

"Humans are stubborn." Jacob complained and then he bowed and the angels left to protect the man I loved.

I looked to my men they were very tired and I asked, "When was the last time that you slept?"

"Awhile" Sayid smiled

"Let's secure shelter and get some food water and much needed rest." Hideki suggested and we found an old abandoned winery in a field a few miles west and we set up camp for the rest of the night.

I didn't sleep, but the men did. When they awoke refreshed I said, "Thank you all for risking your lives to save me."

"Catherine you would have done the same for any of us." Yuri answered.

Sayid added, "You did, and you were only captured because you rescued me."

I smiled, "Are you all ready to make our way toward Peter?" I inquired.

They nodded and we all jogged at a quick pace toward the abandoned church. I felt assured that the angels were already there protecting him, so I was not worried and neither were the men, but we ran anyways.

As we made our way towards Peter, I noticed a large flock of crows flying in a circle above the church. We picked up our pace. When we arrived everyone was engaged in battle with a small group of Satan's soldiers. The where battling for their lives, and for Peter's soul. They encircled Peter.

Peter was shooting many with his pistols, but they had no effect on the warriors, they kept coming despite the number of bullets Peter shot them with.

They advanced quickly into closer range as John blessed some holy water and made a circle around them.

John prayed quietly and then declared, "We are standing on Holy ground they can't cross the barrier."

Peter sighed, "Catherine once told me Satan once sat with her in a church, do really think a little water is going to stop them?"

Peter said this as he lay on the ground to change the angle of his shot and he fired his weapon to ensure the bullet would penetrate the neck and move through the brain of his enemies. It worked, but as the human host died a green mist slithered from the body. Peter kept firing killing several more.

Red mists slithered from the bodies of the larger super soldiers. They made their way like snakes toward Peter.

Peter stood up and backed away from the edge of the circle. The green mists stopped and shrunk back. John declared, "Praise be to God. See Peter, holy ground." As John uttered these words the red snakelike mists reached the circle and slithered across with ease. A Red mist slithered around Peter's body and yet it could not possess him. The mists made their way toward another enemy warrior and inhabited their bodies.

Sky declared, "Peter the ones I kill with the arrow can't inhabit another host. It is as they told us, as if the mists just dissipate instead of trying to travel toward another."

"Then stop talking and keep killing them Sky!"

Peter ordered as he drew his sword gave Kato his dagger.

Kato used the sacred dagger with precision and fluidity killing every demon that approached him as they engaged in hand to hand combat. Kato fought them off with vengeance, while Peter was wielding the sword like a master Samurai.

The angels where fighting a larger group of demon warriors on the hill nearby.

We joined Peter and our men and attacked the demons from behind.

I took my throwing knives and threw them, one after another in rapid succession, as did Hideki, Soku, and Akiro. We threw them each into the back of a soldiers' neck. I was glad I had taken time to retrieve them all back at the castle, including justice that Satan had kept.

Three soldiers fell instantly and the green snake like mists left them and entered into other soldiers nearby. Jacob and his cohorts smiled, for the soldiers taking on new demons were temporarily mesmerized, unable to fight. Sayid took the opportunity to slice their jugulars with his knife and every mortal took on a disabled warrior and killed them. Meanwhile the angels joined us and slashed and fought them with their swords.

I saw Sky shooting my arrows into the enemy as swiftly as he could. The demons that Peter and Sky and Kato killed returned to below and some of the demons realized this and retreated in fear.

Lucifer was angry as he noticed the same thing. He was livid and he yelled, "Enough"

His minions were thankful that their master ceased his attack, for they were losing. I could tell that they were frightened, they could have defeated mortal men and perhaps even angels, if there were enough of the enemy, but God had equipped us with a power they did not comprehend and weapons that when used secured their demise.

Satan addressed the angels. "Arron your god is no longer playing by the rules. These are not mere mortals, and they do not have mortal weapons. If Elohim has equipped them with such power then the agreement is broken. Tell your master that the real war is just beginning."

Arron retorted, "You aren't fooling anyone Lucifer, you waged the war not Elohim. God is restoring the balance, and you know it and I am not your messenger boy. Tell him yourself, if you dare."

I was so elated. Praise be to God. I could not help rejoice and John said, "Our God is almighty and all powerful. He is with us."

Satan knew he could not stand against us when men and angels were united against such a small force, but he retorted, "He is with you for now, but winning a skirmish is not the same as winning a war, Brother John."

Satan smiled and said, "I'll be back for you my queen, and as for you Peter we will definitely see each other again." Then the Devil summoned a flock of crows that the remaining demons entered into.

Satan turned and sped away with the few soldiers he had left with a flock of crows flying in the skies above him back towards the castle.

Lucifer was right the war had just begun. Demons had entered our realm, but we would not face them alone, now that angels walked the earth and fought by our side and the Nephilim bloodline had been revived; we were sure to defeat the Devil's forces. We would win the war, still I was troubled.

I could no longer hide the truth, but I wondered who the Nephilim was that sired my bloodline? I didn't know, nevertheless it was apparent that I was indeed a half-breed.

I would save these apprehensions for another place and time. Besides I didn't need to fret. Our destiny was in the hands of God, as was time itself. Now, I would celebrate that the man who loved me was standing before me and I ran to him, forever grateful to have him in my arms once again.

About The Author

VL Parker has had spiritual encounters throughout her life, while the man she loves never has. Although fictionalized and fantastic for the purpose of entertainment, many of the philosophical and spiritual discussions throughout, **To Hell & Back: A Test of Faith** and **When Angels Walk the Earth,** are based upon real conversations with her spouse.

The author will continue this series and embark on fictionalizing the spiritual truths both ancient and modern. She hopes to use spiritual truths to engage her readers to explore and discuss with others their views in a community of learning.

The tale will continue in a definitive battle between good and evil in **Final Conflict** and **The Secret of Jehovah.**

VL Parker

Made in the USA
Charleston, SC
19 January 2015